MW01002297

The Legacy Collection

Book 1: **Maid for the Billionaire**

Book 2: **For Love or Legacy**

Book 3: **Bedding the Billionaire**

Book 4: **Saving the Sheikh**
Rachid bin Amir al Hantan is fighting for the sovereignty of his small country. He needs to find some powerful allies - and fast. Attending the wedding of Dominic Corisi is as much about reconnecting with old friends as it is about celebrating nuptials. The last thing he needs right now is the distraction of a woman.

Zhang Yajun is a self-made billionaire who can't believe she accepted her friend's dare to kiss Sheikh Rachid before the end of the wedding. When impulsive words lead to even more impulsive actions, these two will discover that sometimes the last thing you were looking for is the one thing that can save you.

Book 5: **Rise of a Billionaire (Spring, 2013)**
Sign up for the mailing list at RuthCardello.com to be notified as soon as Rise of a Billionaire is available.

Saving The

Sheikh

By Ruth Cardello
Copyright © 2012 Ruth Cardello

Author Contact
Website: RuthCardello.com
Email: Minouri@aol.com
Facebook: Author Ruth Cardello
Twitter: RuthieCardello

Dedication:

To Karen and Heather, my two critique partners, who have kindly held my hand and patiently read each chapter no matter how many times I wrote it. To my sister, Helene, who takes time away from her own writing to support mine. To my retired-Marine husband, who now actually enjoys helping me decide what the men would say. And to my three children (Alisha, Victor and Serenity) for understanding that sometimes Mom needs alone time with her laptop.

Also, a special thanks to Caroline Thelemaque, who graciously allowed me to incorporate her story into mine. Caroline advocates for the empowerment and education of women in Haiti and around the world. You can find out more about her and the causes she supports at my website, www.ruthcardello.com. Imagine what would be possible if we all did just a little.

A note to my readers:

Najriad is an imaginary country with a history and set of customs of its own. I used some terms to describe Arab and Chinese attire, but the people and places described in the story are pure fantasy.

Keffiyeh: a traditional Arab headdress fashioned from a square, usually cotton, scarf

Agal: a headband worn by some Arab men to keep the keffiyeh in place

Thobe: a traditional long, Arab tunic

Qipao: a body-hugging one-piece Chinese dress for women

Key characters from previous books:

Dominic Corisi
Nicole Corisi (his sister)

Abby Dartley
Lil Dartley (her sister)
Colby (Lil's infant daughter)
Alethea (Lil's best friend)
Jeremy Kater (Alethea's friend)

Stephan Andrade (Dominic's old rival
and soon to be brother in law)
Antonio Andrade (his father)
Maddy D'Argenson (Stephan's cousin)
Richard D'Argenson (Maddy's husband)

Jake Walton (Dominic's business partner)

Chapter One

Sometimes when you gamble, you lose.

On the small island of Isola Santos, off the coast of Italy, a tuxedo-clad Rachid bin Amir al Hantan stood in the grass to one side of a flower-covered wedding arch, shoulder-to-shoulder with some of the most influential men in the technological world, and attempted to appear interested in the ceremony. Self-recrimination blocked his ability to share in the happiness that was apparent on the face of his old college friend, Dominic Corisi, as he exchanged vows with his bride.

An ocean breeze blew through Rachid's short black hair—highlighting his decision not to wear his traditional keffiyeh headdress. Mocking him. The undeniable truth that he was more at home in Western clothing only intensified his sour mood.

I shouldn't have come.

He spared a glance at the rows of smiling faces and winced. The actual ceremony was a small affair, no more than a hundred or so in attendance, but it was a high-profile wedding and would be talked about for months. Even though the press had been banned, there was no way to keep his participation out of the news.

Which normally wouldn't have been a problem, but Najriad, his home country, was verging on serious political upheaval, and his participation could easily be spun against him—presented as another example of how he didn't care about his people. Even as the wedding crowd laughed over some joke Dominic made in his vows, Najriad's borders were being tested with minor raids. It wouldn't be long before those nips turned to deadly bites.

The same natural resources that had brought them financial

comfort were once again a dangerous temptation for their neighbors. His small country had a strong military and an aggressive political policy that had been enough to keep their enemies at bay for nearly thirty years.

Until Father announced that I would be the one to take his place and called me home.

And no matter what happens, that is what Najriad is—my family, my people, my home.

Even if I am not the ruler they want.

I will do my duty.

I will make my father proud.

Rachid understood his people's concerns. A sheikh was as much a spiritual leader as he was a figure of authority. The title was attained through more than just lineage, and in his absence even his enemies had begun to think that his younger brother, Ghalil, would be ruler one day.

Ghalil had been traditionally educated in Najriad.

He was faithful to the teachings of his people.

And, most importantly, he had never left them.

Not that Rachid had been given a choice. It had been at his father's request that Rachid had left home at the age of eight to attend private schools in England. Amir had asked his son to learn about the technological ways of the West and to bring the best of what he found back to Najriad.

Some who wished to sow dissension between the family members had speculated that Rachid had been sent away so that his father could marry again—and this time produce a full-blooded Arab son, unlike Rachid. Some had whispered that Amir had never forgiven Rachid for his first, English wife dying in childbirth and that Rachid's mere existence had been too much of a reminder of what he had lost.

Whatever his father's reasons, Rachid had excelled in foreign schools, finishing his education at Harvard in the United States. At the time, MIT had seemed like a better choice, but his English relatives had connections to the Cambridge-based Ivy League school, and in the end his attendance had proved to be immensely advantageous.

After all, Harvard was where he'd met Dominic Corisi and Jake Walton. Unlike many he'd encountered, they hadn't cared about his royal title or his country of origin. They had a vision of an empire they wanted to build and it was difficult to spend any time with either of them and not feel inspired to do the same.

The concept for his business, Proximus Solutions, had come from one of their "think tank" sessions; once nothing more than scribbles on the back of a notebook, it now had headquarters all over the world, providing interfacing solutions for countless multibillion-dollar companies. Rachid had intended to base Proximus in Najriad, but opportunity and convenience had caused him to eventually locate its headquarters in Bangalore, India. There had always been a part of him that hoped if he made enough money his people would welcome him again.

Outside of Najriad, he was a wildly successful businessman—both rich and powerful. He didn't second-guess his decisions. His orders were acted upon immediately and without question.

In his country, he was an outsider—someone who spoke English better than he spoke Arabic, appearing socially inept simply because he had grown up outside of his own culture.

The exact opposite of his influential and beloved younger brother.

Money hadn't changed the reality of that.

His father should have chosen Ghalil, but he hadn't. When Rachid had privately questioned his father's choice, the older man had simply said, "Do this for me, son."

That was all Rachid had needed to hear.

A child blissfully allows his parents to carry the burden of the world; a son, a good son, gracefully accepts that burden when it's time for his father to rest.

Family. Responsibility. Loyalty.

Once he would have added faith to that list, but that had

3

RUTH CARDELLO

been another casualty of the crusade his father had sent him on. More nights than he cared to admit, he stared at the ceiling above his bed and wondered what right he had to lead anyone when he himself was lost.

Father, how could I have done everything you've asked of me and still be so wrong?

During an interlude of music, the groomsman next to him pulled Rachid temporarily out of his dark reverie with a question. "So, what do you think of your date?" Richard D'Argenson, the brother-in-law of Dominic's rival, Stephan, had an easy smile that spoke of a lack of stress Rachid couldn't imagine. If this sandstorm ever settled, he'd have to ask Dominic about his odd choice of new friends.

Right now, even the ridiculous was a welcome reprieve from his thoughts. "Excuse me?"

"Zhang Yajun." When he still looked confused, Richard added, "The woman you're going to walk down the aisle with in a moment."

Rachid's attention flew to the beautiful Chinese woman standing beside the three American bridesmaids. Her flawless skin and lovely neck were accentuated by the bun she'd swept her ebony hair up into and her charcoal strapless dress. He sucked in an appreciative breath as he allowed himself the brief indulgence of studying this delicately boned beauty. The tight fit of the dress hugged her small curves in a way every man there likely wanted to. He'd spent enough time in the West to be used to the casual way in which women displayed their bodies. Normally it didn't bother him, but something about this woman made him want to hide her from the leering eyes of other men. He denied the strangely possessive thought.

She's nothing to me.

"Date" was a deliberate exaggeration of what was a temporary pairing for the sake of the ceremony. "I hadn't given her much thought," Rachid said firmly.

"You should," Richard replied.

A woman like Zhang didn't require the Frenchman's

4

endorsement. Women like that only went home alone if they wanted to.

"Really?" he said dismissively. Tempting as she was, there was no room in his life at the moment for a woman. Not tonight. Not in general.

Even one as sexy as Zhang.

She looked at him across the altar and met his eyes, and he felt like he'd been kicked in the abdomen.

Especially one as sexy as Zhang.

Richard said, "The women are hoping there is a love connection there."

Rachid straightened his shoulders. "I'm not interested."

Stephan Andrade whispered back at the two of them. "Keep talking over the officiant and Dominic might just forget that I'm the one he doesn't like."

Rachid glared at the arrogant blond man. He didn't trust Stephan. Vendettas didn't turn off like spigots. Stephan had gone after Dominic for too many years to not still harbor some ill feeling toward him. Was this a case of keeping friends close and enemies closer? Dominic said love had changed Stephan.

Love?

Love was a myth perpetuated by the young and all too often confused with simple lust.

It would take far more than that to change a man's character.

Rachid resolved to keep a close eye on Stephan. Even if he left the wedding with nothing, Rachid owed Dominic that much. He countered the American's joke with a serious warning. "He might forget, but I won't."

The blond's eyes narrowed. "I'm going to enjoy watching you fall."

Rachid stiffened. Was the direness of his situation a topic of global discussion? His face tightened with fury. "Not going to happen."

Stephan smirked and turned away, taunting softly as he did. "You don't know my cousin."

The Frenchman whispered again. "Don't say I didn't warn you. My wife takes matchmaking quite seriously."

Fury left Rachid in a wave. All this chatter was about a woman?

He looked across the aisle again at the stunning self-made billionaire. Richard and Stephan were having fun with him. If they wanted him to believe them, however, they should have picked a more plausible scenario. It was impossible to imagine Zhang giggling like a schoolgirl and plotting against his virtue.

A tiny warrior.

Even in her floor-length gown, she stood with her shoulders squared and her feet planted slightly apart, as if she were braced for a battle. He found the proud set of her chin and the direct way her eyes met his when she caught him looking at her surprisingly sexy.

I'd love to kiss the fight right out of her.

She smiled at him as if she could hear his thoughts, and he straightened uncomfortably in response to the heat rushing through him. If not for the jacket of his tuxedo, everyone gathered might have seen the effect she was having on him.

He returned his attention to the happy, newly married couple.

It was bad enough that Dominic and Jake were hopelessly absorbed in the women they were with, leaving very little opportunity for Rachid to talk business with them. He had to return with something that would prove to his people that his time away had not been wasted. Money wasn't enough—he had to show his people he had the connections to support the type of technological infrastructure he'd proposed. A contract with Dominic's Corisi Enterprises would do that.

I still have time.

It's often the last key in the bunch that opens the door.

The wedding isn't over yet.

He glanced at Zhang, felt his chest tighten in excited response, and quickly looked away again. *If I don't let her distract me.*

One by one the other groomsmen joined a bridesmaid, following Dominic and his new bride down the aisle. Zhang linked her arm with Rachid's and smiled up at him from beneath thick, flirtatious lashes.

He scowled down at the temptation.

Zhang's hand tightened on his arm, and he would have sworn that her jaw set with determination as she looked away.

Zhang Yajun knew that her attention should be on the ceremony being performed a few feet away from her, but her heart was racing in her chest and her eyes were repeatedly drawn to the dark-haired groomsman on the other side of the aisle.

Rachid bin Amir al Hantan, crown prince of Najriad— easily the most attractive man she'd ever seen and the only one she'd ever pinkie-sworn to kiss.

Lil, why did I let you talk me into this?

If she were honest, it wasn't her new friend's fault. It had taken Zhang just one look into those beautiful black eyes—even when they had been only digitally displayed on a wall-length screen, during Abby's bachelorette party—to realize that years of neglect didn't stop genitalia from functioning.

So much for using it or losing it.

Hers was a case of damming it up the best she could for years and then feeling ridiculous when a photo was enough to make her thighs quiver. Celibacy must be its own type of insanity. There was no other explanation for why a self-made, successful businesswoman would be staring longingly across an aisle at a perfect stranger, like a schoolgirl hoping her first crush would notice her, and periodically smiling at him even though he didn't return the overture.

And why would he?

Men like Rachid aren't attracted to women like me. Any of the women standing next to me probably would have a hundred percent better chance of gaining his attention. Forget how

7

radiant Abby was as a bride: Her sister, Lil, exuded a sexual confidence that made men stand straighter when she entered a room. Nicole Corisi, the groom's sister, had a cool, feminine sophistication—stunning in a way few women were. Even Maddy, Stephan's young cousin who had recently given birth, had a playful little-sister appeal that brought out the protective side in men.

And what do I have?

The ability to back down even the most aggressive opponent.

Wow, that's sexy.

I can sense a market trend months before others can and make millions practically in my sleep.

That and a calculator puts me at... what... negative four on a sex scale?

Zhang groaned.

I wasn't always like this.

There had been a time, long ago, when she had laughed, tucked into a lover's embrace, and felt sexy and invincible. Until that love had demanded that she choose—and she had.

A fork in the road. One way had led to a life she'd been able to imagine every day of, and the other to one that had promised real struggle—but also the possibility of satisfying a need that had always burned within her.

Even as a young woman, Zhang had wanted to see everything and learn as much as she could, and she'd sworn to one day improve the living conditions of her family and her countrywomen. Lofty goals for someone born into poverty in a small Chinese village.

Goals she had thought Xin Yui understood. In his first year of university, they had spent many hours passionately debating the topics from his courses.

And making love.

Young and foolish.

If anyone had discovered their secret, Zhang would have paid a hefty price of both shame and punishment.

On what was easily the worst night of her life, Xin had begged her to run away with him. He'd wanted to marry quickly and return to his parents' home together. He'd saved enough money to make the generous gifts that would win her parents' forgiveness for their impulsive actions.

All she had to do was say yes.

Yes to putting her dreams aside.

Yes to a life she had been raised to respect.

It should have been an easy decision. This was what women did when they married. Their focus became their new husband, his family and the child they created together. At eighteen, many of her friends were married. Some had a son or daughter already. She'd thought it was what she also wanted until Xin had asked and a voice in her heart had screamed a refusal.

No to putting her dreams aside.

No to the life she had been raised to respect.

No to Xin.

Not a single one of her friends understood her decision. She'd tried to explain to them that she wasn't passing judgment on their life choices. At first they had been worried for her, but concern became anger, and they'd lashed out as if her decision somehow threatened their own. The women in her family distanced themselves from her. Her own mother refused to speak to her for months.

Xin must have truly loved her, because he didn't give up easily. He waited for her until he could wait no longer. Out of desperation, he had gone and spoken to her father, hoping the well-respected elder could persuade Zhang to marry him.

In a move that had shaken his standing in the community, Zhang's father had defended her right to choose her path. Despite a public backlash—or perhaps because of it—he had taken the family's savings and sent Zhang to the city to go to university. His support was selfless, and it had amplified Zhang's drive to succeed. Whenever she'd doubted herself, she thought of what her father had risked for her to have her chance.

It had taken her five years to make enough money to move her parents out of their small village and into a modest home in the city. Only a few more years before they had homes all over the world and private planes to take them wherever they wanted to go.

Long ago, Zhang had surpassed even what she'd dreamt she could become. She had more money than she could spend in a thousand lifetimes, and enough political influence to enact policy changes that would improve the lives of millions of Chinese women.

So why am I not happy?

Why am I grasping at a pinkie-sworn kiss like it could change my life?

Because I'm alone.

The universe had a way of sending messages and opportunities. Most people didn't allow themselves to hear them. Zhang was keenly attuned to these nudges and credited her success to that gift.

Lil's words were a divine dare—a price demanded for a second chance at love. The ocean breeze whispered, *Prove that you want it and it can be yours.*

Cheering announced the end of the ceremony Zhang should have been paying attention to. Dominic Corisi and his new bride reluctantly broke off their passionate kiss and led the way down the aisle. One by one, bridesmaids linked arms with groomsmen and followed the newly married couple.

Lil Dartley and Jake Walton.

Nicole Corisi and Stephan Andrade.

Maddy and her husband, Richard D'Argenson.

Zhang held her breath and stepped forward, linking her arm with Rachid's. She peeked up at him from beneath her lashes and offered him a sweet smile.

He scowled down at her.

Zhang's hand tightened on her escort's well-muscled arm.

You're not going to make it easy, universe?

Fine.

Get my happily-ever-after ready, because this is one sheikh who is going to be kissed before midnight.

Chapter Two

"Please follow me," requested one of the tuxedo-clad wedding staff as Rachid and Zhang exited the large white tent. "The bride and groom are taking pictures and have requested that you join them outside for just a few moments." He led the way to a shaded area near the ocean bluffs.

When they came to a stop, Zhang knew she should let go of Rachid's arm, but she didn't. She didn't need forever from this man. *Just one kiss. How hard could that be?*

Rachid leaned down and spoke softly into her ear. "I must apologize for not getting here early enough to practice the ceremony with you. My tardiness delayed our formal introduction, something we can rectify now. My name is Rachid."

"I know," she said breathlessly and stopped, realizing she'd revealed too much in those few words. "My name is Zhang."

"Yes," he said vaguely. Suddenly looking as annoyed as he had earlier.

I really should let go of his arm.

Not yet.

"I didn't know you had a British accent," Zhang said in her own stilted English. His fluency implied he'd learned the language at a much younger age than she had.

"I attended Eton," he said dismissively, as if his years at one of England's most prestigious preparatory schools was something he preferred to forget.

"Your English is native-like."

His features tightened. "A byproduct of living there for more than a decade."

"Quite useful, I'm sure."

"Less so than you'd think," he said vaguely.

They fell into a short and awkward silence. Zhang willed herself to relax.

Remain casual.

Cool.

Make light conversation.

"Crown prince of Najriad—that can't be easy, considering the amount of unrest in that area right now."

His head pulled back and he straightened. "I'd rather not discuss it," he said abruptly. His arm dropped away in a not-so-subtle withdrawal.

Zhang wanted to stomp her foot in frustration, but she kept her features composed and her feet still.

Universe 1
Zhang 0

Ok, so I'm rusty when it comes to flirting.

Note to self: Politics is not a sexy topic.

Zhang took a fortifying breath.

If I can inspire loyalty from what was once a purely mercenary security force, surely I can win over one man long enough to get a kiss.

Zhang laid a hand on Rachid's forearm to regain his attention. With a forced flutter of her eyelashes, she said huskily, "I hope I didn't upset you."

"You didn't," he said. He cleared his throat and once again gently pulled his arm away from her. "I need a drink. Would you like one?"

Zhang answered automatically and then corrected herself. "I don't—yes, fine. Thank you."

He walked away with insulting speed.

Universe 2
Zhang 0

Reality was not living up to her fantasy. She'd barely exchanged two words with him and already her escort had fled.

Where was the hot-blooded, passionate sheikh who had haunted her dreams since Maddy had shown her a picture of how he would look at her side today? Flashes of the two of them beneath silken sheets, exploring, teasing, brought a heat to Zhang's face as she watched Rachid cross the grassy area to where a server stood with a tray of champagne.

From head to toe, Rachid was perfection. Thick locks battled against a conservative cut in a gloriously rebellious way that made a woman want to run her fingers through his hair and unlock his inner wild side. Even in his formal Western attire Rachid had an exotic and untamed aura about him. Zhang watched Stephan Andrade approach him and compared the two men. Both were tall with broad shoulders that their tuxes only emphasized. However, next to Rachid's striking dark skin, black hair and brooding eyes, the blond American looked pale and one-dimensional.

Her pulse quickened. *How could you not imagine a man like that naked?*

I should've been a painter. They can get away with asking strangers to take off their clothes.

Zhang chewed her bottom lip and wondered if Rachid measured up against Stephan as favorably in other places that were presently hidden. An uncharacteristic chuckle escaped her before Zhang reined herself in.

I need professional help.

Or one night with that man.

Giving herself a mental shake, Zhang corrected her inner voice.

Not a night, just a kiss.

The longer the two men spoke, the more Zhang began to feel a bit ridiculous. She wasn't a wild teenager, caving to an impulsive dare in the face of peer pressure. Nor was she some desperate woman who needed a man to make her life complete.

What am I doing?

I've made it this far alone.

I should just forget this whole stupid idea.

A voice whispered in her mind, *Fear is failure's best friend.*

I'm not afraid.

She squared her shoulders. Another woman would have given up in the face of Rachid's rather cold response to her attempts to gain his attention. However, another woman might not have taken every no she'd ever heard as a dare and made her fortune proving that tenacity and bold action equated to success.

I'm not afraid, she reaffirmed to herself.

And I'll prove it.

On any other day, the promise in Zhang's heated glances would have been enough to pique Rachid's interest. However, they were an unwelcome temptation that day.

He didn't like the way his skin warmed and tingled beneath the slight touch of her hand. He resented how aware he was of each move she made, even now that he'd put some distance between them. He'd had his share of sophisticated lovers over the years, but none had made his heart race at the mere thought of looking at her again.

Oh, no, Zhang Yajun was a dangerous distraction.

One who refused to be ignored.

Her attempts to pull him into conversation had been endearingly awkward. He'd been tempted to tell her so, but he'd bitten back the words, aware that they might have led to a more comfortable exchange. Today was about Najriad, not satisfying some carnal desire that would only put him in a worse standing with his people if it were uncovered.

He was in the process of taking a glass of champagne from a server when Stephan approached. A quick look around confirmed that Dominic was still holding his new bride to his side for the photographer and that Jake Walton and his woman were missing again.

Stephan stopped a foot or so away and pocketed his hands casually. "I thought about what you said back there, and I wanted to reassure you that Dominic and I have put our differences behind us."

Rachid didn't hide his scorn. "Time and actions reveal intentions more accurately than words."

Stephan conceded the point with a slight inclination of his head. He looked over at Dominic and back at Rachid. "I didn't realize that you knew Dominic so well. Jake said you all met back in college."

"A fact that is hardly a secret."

"No, but considering how long it has been since you've been seen with him, it makes me wonder if you came here today for old time's sake or for some other reason."

"I can assure you that my reasons for attending this wedding are none of your concern."

True to his reputation, Stephan didn't take the hint. "Andrade Global is now an affiliate of Corisi Enterprises. Instead of going home empty-handed, you might want to consider that."

"I didn't come here to talk business, Stephan."

"Didn't you?" Stephan smiled confidently. "Dominic will be gone on his honeymoon for at least a week, and Jake has temporarily checked out. When they return, they'll both be busy with the scheduled Chinese server project. Andrade Global is your best viable option. Think about it." He held out his business card.

Rachid ignored it. "Why the interest, Stephan?"

Stephan's hand dropped to his side. "I admire what you're trying to do for Najriad."

"Your approval is of no importance to me."

Stephan's smile shifted to a knowing grin. "But my ability to land you the type of high-profile contract you're looking for is."

"I am here to honor an old friendship."

"Don't let your pride cost you the win, Rachid. I may not

be your first choice, but can you afford to leave here with nothing?" He offered the card to Rachid again.

Rachid pocketed it reluctantly. He would have loved to throw that card right back into Stephan's face, but he had a sinking feeling that the man was right. Even a rat eventually looked appetizing to a starving man. "Your instincts are good. When would you like to discuss this further?"

"I can fly out to meet with you on Tuesday."

"I will be in Nilon in my father's palace."

"Perfect." Beginning to turn away, Stephan stopped and added, "Tuesday, then."

Rachid reached for another glass of champagne. There were many things he wanted to say to the overly smug man, but he held his tongue. His country just might need him. "Tuesday."

Stephan added, "Hey, and good luck with Zhang. My guess is that you'll need it."

Rachid didn't dignify the comment with a response. He turned with both glasses in hand and headed back toward Zhang with a lighter step.

No, he hadn't gotten Corisi Enterprises to offer a contract, but Stephan's offer brought more relief than he cared to admit. A small press release could announce the possible alliance with Andrade Global and justify his temporary absence. He didn't want to get too hopeful, but the right contract, even with someone like Stephan, might improve his public image and could go a long way in helping to stabilize the borders. His people needed a reason to believe in him. He hoped this would be the first step toward winning their trust.

Either way, there is nothing more that can be done tonight.

Time to relax a bit and perhaps enjoy the evening. As he approached Zhang, she backed away from him and disappeared around the corner of the large white tent.

Now what is that woman up to?

Not following her didn't even occur to him.

17

Just do it.

Zhang planted her feet firmly in the lush grass. No turning back now.

What if he doesn't follow me?

Shaking off the negative question, Zhang reminded herself that nothing positive came from worrying about what might not happen. Success came from charging forward. Or, in the words of the American motivational speaker Tony Robbins, from taking "massive, determined action."

That's what this situation needed before their reason for standing together disappeared and she lost what might have been her only chance. One kiss and her side of the bargain would be done.

She held her breath and waited.

Light footsteps approached.

Her heart jumped in her chest when Rachid stepped around the corner of the tent and into the privacy the temporary cloth alley created. His brows met in question as he walked toward her. "Zhang?" he asked, his tone concerned, a glass of champagne still in either hand.

She closed the distance between them with a few determined strides and grabbed him by the lapels of his tux, pulling him down toward her. She grated, "I'm done trying to be subtle. Let's just get this over with."

Rising to her tiptoes, she met his lips with a force that stunned them both for a moment.

Heat exploded between them, and what was supposed to be a brief touch lingered. After only the slightest hesitation, his mouth settled on hers and began a quest of its own. His tongue teased, then plundered.

As her knees buckled beneath her, Zhang was suddenly steadying herself against Rachid rather than pulling him to her. Drowning beneath a wave of passion, she forgot the wedding, forgot the dare, and left the world behind. The thud of glasses dropping to the ground was followed by the heavenly feeling of Rachid's hands closing around her waist and pulling her closer.

His lips moved across her cheek and down her neck, his hot breath tickling as it excited.

Impatiently, her hands sought more of him. They slid beneath his jacket and closed around the warm muscles of his back. His mouth returned to hers, demanding a submission that she gave gladly as he lifted her off her feet and the kiss intensified.

The sound of the wedding planner calling for them brought Zhang quickly back to reality.

She turned her head to one side, breaking the kiss off, and took a shaky breath. "You can put me down now," she said.

"I could," he said, and smiled against her neck.

Awkward didn't begin to describe how she felt. She could only imagine what he thought of her. "Put me down," she said coldly.

He eased her gently back onto her feet but didn't release her. "If you wanted to get my attention, you have it now."

Zhang squirmed a bit in his embrace, but his hold only tightened on her. "They're looking for us."

He nuzzled her ear and she shuddered. "Let them look."

She put her hands between the two of them and pushed against him a bit. "You may have gotten the wrong impression of me."

He raised his head and studied her upturned face. "I don't think so. You're an incredibly intelligent, spirited woman who takes what she wants." One of his hands shifted down to span the small of her back. "I could enjoy that for a night."

With one firm shove, Zhang pushed away from him. "Thanks for the offer, but I must decline. All I needed was the kiss." She straightened her clothing. In response to the surprise in his face, she said, "You wouldn't understand." She stepped toward escape.

He blocked her path. "Try me."

Ignoring how his nearness sent flutters through her stomach, Zhang said, "If you must know, it was a dare."

He grabbed her wrist, the lines of his face becoming harsh.

"Like a joke?"

She tried and failed to free herself from his grasp. "No, not a joke. It was supposed to—I really can't explain it. All I can do is say that weddings make women a little crazy." She sent him a harassed glare. "Can we leave it at that?"

He turned her hand over in his. "You intrigue me, Zhang Yajun. Is this normal for you, or am I your first wedding ambush?"

Her cheeks warmed with embarrassment. "What are the chances we could forget this happened?"

"Pretty close to zero."

"And what exactly is it going to take to get you to let go of my arm?"

He smiled and said, "I'd settle for an explanation." When she let out a relieved breath he laughed, "What were you thinking the price would be?"

Zhang couldn't help it—she returned his smile. "You have a dirty mind."

His smile widened. "Says the woman who jumped an unsuspecting man who had simply come back here to make sure she was okay."

She rolled her eyes and laughed. "Poor man."

"Lucky man," he said softly, and she blushed again. With a tug, he pulled her against him. She craned her neck back to look up at his face, the wild beating of their hearts synchronizing. "Are you going to tell me, or should I kiss it out of you?"

Zhang gulped.

Tough choice.

Her body quivered in anticipation even as her mind listed all the reasons why a hasty retreat was the wisest option. "How do you know you'd succeed?"

He leaned down until their lips almost touched and said, "The fun would be in trying."

Yes, it would be.

A glimmer of sanity returned.

No, it would not.

This has already gone too far.

Maybe a little honesty was just what this situation needed. "I wanted to prove something to myself."

"And did you?" he asked in a whisper.

Yes, that all of my bits and pieces are still functioning perfectly, even if my brain is temporarily on the fritz. "Yes," she whispered back.

"You really want to end this with one kiss?"

She wondered how many women had melted and surrendered when he'd asked that question in that husky tone. She was sure she didn't want to know. The thought of him with another woman gave her the strength to resist. "It seems like the wisest course of action."

Rachid shook his head in mock disappointment. "I thought you were braver than that, Zhang."

"You don't even know me."

"I'd like to."

"For one night."

His expression sobered. "I don't have more than that to offer."

Honestly, neither did she, at least not to a man who had his own overwhelming amount of responsibility. She may have, in a moment or two of weakness, researched the prince online. What had stemmed from mere curiosity had become more intense as she'd learned more about his country. Anything long-term between them was out of the question. He would never relocate, and she couldn't imagine herself in his country any more than she could imagine herself moving back to her old village. Still, what woman wouldn't be tempted by a gorgeous and confident man like Rachid? Unlike so many of the men she met who wanted something either financial or political from her, Rachid was promising her a night of mutual pleasuring without asking for anything in return. No strings. No regrets. Tempting, but not a wise choice. "It would be incredibly reckless."

He ran a hand gently over one of her cheeks. "Why don't

we start by simply enjoying the wedding together."

Although it was highly unlikely that more time with this man was going to make the decision easier, Zhang was powerless to deny him. "I could do that."

His hands slid lower, closing over the curve of her behind and pulling her against his excitement. "The cost of your freedom is one kiss."

"You said it was an explanation."

"I changed my mind," he murmured and his lips descended down onto hers again—testing.

Instantly, feverishly, they clung to each other. His strong hands lifted her to fit her more tightly against him. Had it not been for the length of her gown, she would have wrapped her legs around his waist. As it was, their clothing did little to stop either of them from exploring.

With an expletive Zhang didn't understand, Rachid set her back from him and said, "Come, let's return to the wedding before I lose control and take you here on the grass."

Not exactly a threat when I've considered doing the same.

Zhang quickly collected her thoughts and kept her features tightly controlled. If she was careful, she could spend an amazing and passionately charged evening with this incredible man and call it to a halt before it went too far. A few kisses. A little flirtation. Isn't that what Lil said happened at an American wedding? Hadn't she been careful long enough? She'd denied herself anything intimate and kept her focus on her business. What would one evening hurt as long as no one knew? "You go first. I don't want anyone to know we were alone back here."

Rachid looked down at her quickly. "Concerned about your reputation?"

His question stung. People made assumptions about her and her morality based on her lifestyle. Normally she shrugged it off as a price she paid for being free. She wanted—needed—Rachid to understand. "I may live by my own rules, but I have a family and I won't dishonor them. "

He touched her cheek again softly. "Anything we do will

be discrete. I promise you that." When she opened her mouth to respond to him, he gently placed one finger over her lips and said, "And if nothing happens at all, my opinion of you will remain the same—you are one fascinating woman, Zhang."

A female voice called out from a short distance. "Zhang? Are you back here?"

Damn.

Zhang looked into those amazing black eyes and said, "That's Lil. She shouldn't find us like this."

After one last brief kiss, Rachid nodded his agreement and walked away in the opposite direction of Lil's voice.

Zhang let out a long breath and brought a shaky hand to her mouth, savoring the lingering warmth of his touch.

If this is a dream, don't wake me up yet.

Lil bounded around the tent and stopped dead when she saw Zhang. "There you are! Abby wants a picture with the whole wedding party and no one could find you."

Zhang straightened her dress and boldly lied. "I needed a moment alone."

Instantly, Lil's expression changed and she swept closer, making Zhang regret her choice of excuses. "I'm so sorry. I know how you feel about weddings."

A secret smile tugged at the corners of Zhang's lips. *I may have just changed my opinion of them.* "Please do not be concerned, Lil. I'm fine."

Lil looked around, saw the glasses of champagne at Zhang's feet and drew her own conclusion. "I'm an ass. I shouldn't have dared you to kiss that sheikh. It was childish and stupid. Forget I even said it."

Real concern clouded her friend's eyes and tore at Zhang's composure. This wasn't fun if it hurt someone. "It wasn't childish, Lil. You wanted to give me a reason to smile today and you did."

Lil countered, "Really? Then why are you hiding back here drinking by yourself?"

"I wasn't..."

23

Lil shook her head sadly, clearly not believing her. After all, the evidence was at her feet.

"I was with Rachid."

Lil's jaw dropped open. "The sheikh?"

Zhang kept her expression serene, although some amusement filtered into her tone. "Is there more than one here tonight?"

A slow grin swept all worry from the brunette's face. "Holy crap! You kissed him, didn't you?"

Zhang nodded, a proud smile bursting forth.

Lil hopped in excitement and hugged her. "You are one hot shit, Zhang! I love it!"

Pulling back slightly from her overexuberant friend, Zhang repeated the label. "Hot shit." She mulled the term. "I can't say I've been called that before. It's a compliment?"

Lil was practically dancing with excitement and might have hugged her again had Zhang not taken another step back. She enjoyed Lil, but the constant touching was something she wasn't quite used to.

Lil said, "From me, it's a huge one. You're my new hero."

Now I know I'm in trouble.

Suddenly sobering a bit, Zhang asked, "Can we keep this between the two of us?"

"Absolutely," Lil said. She linked arms with Zhang and together they started walking toward the wedding party. "I can keep a secret."

Zhang paused, causing Lil to come to an abrupt halt beside her, and simply looked up at her until the younger woman blushed.

"When it's important," Lil qualified.

Zhang's eyebrows rose in challenge.

"Do you want me to pinkie-swear?" Lil asked in growing offense.

Zhang started walking again, but this time she was smiling. "No, one per wedding is all I can handle."

Lil hugged Zhang's arm to her side and laughed as they

strolled together. She added in a stage whisper, "I can't believe you did it."

Lil's enthusiasm was impossible to resist. A light laugh burst from her as Zhang conceded, "I can't either." She gave her friend's arm a slight squeeze. No matter how the evening ended, Zhang had taken a risk, and the result was that she felt more alive and hopeful than she had in years. Life shouldn't be a story about what the world did with you; it should be about what you did with the world. "Thank you."

Nearing the grassy area where the wedding party was already standing in position, waiting to complete the photos, Zhang couldn't help but sneak a look at Rachid. He was standing with the other groomsmen on one side of Dominic. Composed. Looking every bit the visiting monarch he was.

Lil announced, "I found Zhang! She was..." Her hesitation hung heavy in the silence as everyone waited. "Lost," she finished lamely.

All eyes flew to Zhang. *Thanks, Lil, now people are wondering if I'm drunk.* Agreeing was easier than attempting another cover story, so she shrugged and concurred, "So many tents that all look alike."

Abby broke the awkward pause that followed. She waved Lil and Zhang toward her side. "Well, come on! We've been waiting for you. Get over here. Just a few more photos and then we can go eat."

Lil took her spot near her sister.

Zhang headed toward the other bridesmaids, looking over at Rachid one last time as she joined them. His expression gave nothing away as he stared back at her. It would be easy enough to convince herself that she had imagined the entire alley exchange.

He was right to pretend nothing had happened.

Nothing had.

Not really.

Just one meaningless kiss.

Better forgotten.

25

Then Rachid winked at her and the photographer recorded Zhang's happy responding flush.

In the words of one expressive American: *Holy crap*.

Chapter Three

Seated chastely with the bridal party at a large, round table in the enormous white main tent, Zhang laid her napkin across her lap. Everywhere she looked there was a combination of practical and bold design. The table decorations were simple crystal vases of white orchids that complemented the enormous size of the tent and the opulence of the hanging chandeliers. It was easy to distinguish which ideas had come from the bride and which had come from the groom. The blend of both of their styles was a lovely and impressive display of their love.

Abby had taken great care to ensure the comfort of their guests. Each glass was adorned with handmade stem jewelry, and each place card held a personalized message on the back. Most likely Abby had chosen the words and Dominic had chosen the diamonds. Both were something the guests would treasure. Everyone else at her table was focused on the bride and groom performing their first dance as a married couple, but regardless of how she tried to distract herself, Zhang was finding it difficult to concentrate on anything but the man beside her.

Rachid whispered in her ear. "I thought your dress was floor-length."

The tickle of his breath on her neck sent a naughty shiver down her spine. She defended the wardrobe change, even though she knew from the light in his eyes that he wasn't complaining. "The bottom was detachable and meant to be removed after the ceremony."

He raised one eyebrow playfully.

She shook her head with slight smile. "That's the only piece that comes off."

"Pity," he said, and her heart beat double-time at the sexy purse of his lips.

Zhang turned her attention to the newly married couple. This was normally the point where she would have made excuses and ended the night early. There was only so much happily ever after a person could stomach when her own life was an emotional desert. Tonight was different. For the first time, watching two people publicly and repeatedly proclaim their love for each other didn't sadden Zhang.

I determine my path. I can have love if I choose it. Tonight is not about sleeping with an Arab sheikh, it's about opening my heart to possibilities. The past doesn't determine my future.

I'm finally free.

The groom's sister, Nicole, gracefully stood and took Stephan by the hand. "This is where we join them on the dance floor."

Maddy and Richard rose from their seats. Both couples turned to look at Zhang and Rachid.

Zhang shook her head quickly and remained seated. "I don't dance."

Maddy said, "Oh, but you have to! Abby will be so disappointed if we don't all join her. Where is Lil?"

Perfect excuse!

Zhang stood and hastily offered, "I'll go look for her."

Rachid also stood, held out a hand to her and said, "I'm sure she and Jake would rather have a moment alone."

An inner battle ensued. She wanted nothing more than to be in Rachid's arms again, but not like this, not in public—and certainly not while displaying her complete lack of dance experience. "I don't—"

Bending to her ear so that his words would be heard only by her, Rachid said, "Tonight you do."

His eyes burned with a desire for more than a dance. It held a question she wasn't prepared to answer yet.

"One dance," she answered huskily, heat from the pleasure she read in his expression spreading through her abdomen and lower. She took the hand he offered and followed him onto the dance floor, trying to ignore the knowing expressions on the faces of those in their group.

Once on the dance floor, Zhang was careful to keep an acceptable distance between them as they swayed to the slow ballad. Rachid placed a hand on her waist, intending to pull her closer, but when she tensed he relaxed his hold and allowed the space between them to remain.

He bent to once again whisper in her ear. "Where is the bold woman who takes what she wants?"

She smiled sadly up at him, hating that she felt awkward before him. She was certainly that person when it came to business, but in private matters she had closed herself off for so long that she still felt unsure. "If I were that woman, I wouldn't have needed the dare."

"You're a dangerous combination of everything I like in a woman," he said. In response to the skeptical expression on her face, he asked, "That surprises you?"

"I would have thought your taste ran more toward submissive women."

"And what do you know of my preferences?"

"You're right. I guess I let your title shape my fantasies," she admitted, instantly wanting to retract the words. *I don't know why I said that.*

If her goal had been to test the level of his interest, she wasn't disappointed. His hand tightened on her waist. "Fantasies?" The sudden heat in his eyes was everything Zhang would have wished for—if she'd let herself make such wishes.

Passion without love was wrong.

But was it more wrong than spending a lifetime without intimacy? Never feeling the brush of a kiss on your shoulder? Never knowing the warm touch of a lover? A decade of celibacy was a hefty price to pay for success and duty.

One evening. That's all I ask. A few hours that have nothing to do with the life I must maintain or the one I left behind. Give me the words that will keep this man interested long enough to make a memory that I can savor when I return home alone tonight. She said, "You have to know that many women fantasize about Arab sheikhs."

Now he did pull her closer, and this time she didn't resist. "I don't care about women in general, but you have this fantasy?"

She studied his chest for a moment, then boldly met his eyes. "Yes."

"Tell me."

She looked down again, suddenly feeling unsure. She should tell him now that she had no intention of sleeping with him that evening. Continuing the conversation would only lead him to believe that she wanted him.

Not that I don't want him, but wanting and acting are two completely different things. I must end this now before things get awkward.

She hedged as she sought the strength to walk away. "It's silly, really."

There was nothing silly about the need she saw in his eyes as he raised her chin with one finger. "Tell me."

The universe whispered, *Prove that you want it, Zhang. Be brave.*

Zhang squared her delicate shoulders and said, "The slightly unwilling virgin being swept away to a desert castle by a hot-blooded sheikh and forced to pleasure him."

His head tipped to one side. "Forced?"

She shrugged. "It's a fantasy. No one gets hurt in a fantasy."

He massaged her lower back as he contemplated what she had shared. "That's it?"

In for penny, in for a pound. She smiled wickedly and added, "Hardly. There is something about those harem outfits and silk pillows." She shuddered in response to a wave of sexual excitement coursing through her. "I know it's outdated and a Hollywood stereotype, but it doesn't change how fun it is to imagine."

When Zhang glanced up at Rachid's face she expected to see him laughing, but he wasn't. His serious expression worried her.

I hope I didn't offend him.

"Are you a virgin?" he asked softly.

She gulped and met his eyes proudly. "No."

His smile was completely unexpected—and devastatingly sexy. He spun her around, catching her fully against him, and growled into her ear, "Good."

Well, that could be taken a thousand ways, and not many of them flattering. Never one to play coy, Zhang demanded, "What exactly is that supposed to mean?"

"I have no respect for men who take advantage of innocence, but I want to be with you tonight, Zhang." Their dance came to a sudden halt and he simply stared down at her. A playful but oh-so-sexually charged fire lit his eyes. "And I have a desert castle."

Zhang would have slid to the floor if Rachid hadn't caught her.

Holy crap.

Nothing about being with Zhang was a good idea.

And yet, she was all that mattered to Rachid when he held her in his arms.

Many women had thrown themselves at him over the years—money and a title tended to do that for a man. Some had been subtle, some obvious, and a few had even played hard to get. He liked to think that their time together had been mutually satisfying, if not earth-shattering. History was stained with wars born from lust for a woman. He'd always scoffed at the feasibility of any woman having such power over a man.

Until Zhang had shared her fantasy with him and lit a need in him that swelled and choked out all reason. Tonight he didn't want to be a successful businessman or dutiful son. He didn't want to carry the weight of his people or the expectations of his family.

Tonight he wanted to lose himself in this woman and her fantasy.

One night.

She knew he couldn't offer her more than that.

If she accepted his offer, he would savor every moment of it.

Rather than pretending to eat the meal that had been served shortly after they returned to their table, Rachid excused himself and stepped out of the tent. He needed a private area to prepare for the possibility that Zhang might say yes.

He took out his cell phone and called the main number of the castle at the Salnyra Oasis. The once-abandoned ancient building had been lovingly restored by his grandfather and was now a mixture of history and modern luxury. Generators provided electricity for rooms that had once been occupied by Roman soldiers. Faded frescos that had been drawn for nomadic Bedouin sheikhs of the past covered the walls of a castle that was now more a vacation home than a defensive structure. When one of the manservants answered, Rachid said, "I will be flying in late tonight. Please have the airfield lights on." He realized too late that he'd issued the order in English.

The man responded in Arabic, even though he spoke English. "As you wish, Your Highness."

It was difficult to imagine being able to rule his country when he hadn't yet successfully won over the house staff. Another problem that could wait one more day.

"Also, I need you to prepare the old harem quarters for me."

"It will be done."

Rachid hesitated, then charged on. "I'd like most of the furniture removed from the rooms and replaced with as many silk pillows as will cover the floor."

"Your Highness?"

He took a moment to consider what Zhang might have imagined, then instructed, "Hang tapestries from the ceiling to mimic the inside of a Bedouin tent. Tie them back with silk scarves."

"Anything else?"

A thought came to him and he snapped his fingers in the air. "Yes, I need a harem outfit. Something expensive, but similar to what a belly dancer might wear. And a dress that would be appropriate for daywear."

"For you, Your Highness?"

"No," Rachid said impatiently. "For a woman. A small woman."

"Of course, Your Highness."

"And no one is to disturb me until noon tomorrow."

"It will be as you ask."

Yes, it will be.

For one night, at least.

Chapter Four

Inside of every man there's a hunter who hides beneath layers of learned civilized behavior. Returning to the dining tent and discovering that Zhang hadn't waited at the table for him, something primal woke within Rachid. He scanned the room and adrenaline coursed through him when he realized that she wasn't there.

She wasn't going to make it easy for him.

He hardened instantly.

I like the way this woman thinks.

She wasn't in any of the other tents, nor was she in the area between them. The more he looked for her, the less he could deny his growing excitement.

I will find you, Zhang, and then I will have you.

When he finally spotted her on the isolated balcony of Dominic's main house, he had to restrain himself from sprinting to her. Never before had he engaged in such behavior. He met women, dated them, bedded them and moved on.

He didn't play games.

He couldn't deny, though, that this particular scenario was extremely pleasurable. He moved through the shadows around the balcony and kept his steps silent as he approached her. Waiting until he was less than a foot behind her, he said softly, "Hiding only delays the inevitable."

She turned quickly toward him and snarled, "My father had no right to give me to you! I will not go with you!"

His head pulled back in surprise as he realized that she was playing a role. Then he smiled—an "oh, yes, this is going to be fun" smile. He reached for her waist and pulled her toward him.

She slapped him clear across the face. The sting was

surprisingly real and gave an edge to her fantasy. His hands clenched on her sides.

Instantly, her expression filled with concern and she touched the red mark she'd left on his face. "Oh, my God, I didn't mean to hit you so hard. I just thought that if you really were here to kidnap me, I wouldn't fall willingly into your arms."

Rachid threw his head back and laughed, the tension of his daily life falling away temporarily. He covered her hand on his cheek with his and said, "How about we make a deal to keep actual pain to a minimum."

She laughed up into his eyes. "You must think I'm insane."

He pulled her closer and spoke from his heart. "No, I think you are the sexiest woman I've ever met. Tonight is exactly what I need—I just don't want either one of us to take it too far. Exactly what are you looking for?"

Zhang looked down at his shirt, then met his eyes again and said, "My experience is limited, but I've had a lifetime to dream about what I like. I know this is only for one night. Tomorrow will come and I'll be alone again. I'm okay with that. But for just one night, I want to pretend something entirely different."

Touching her hair softly, he said, "If we had met in another time or another life, I would have more than one night to offer. I don't want to hurt you, Zhang. You deserve more than this."

Those beautiful, intelligent eyes pierced his soul. "Are you backing out?"

God help him, he couldn't.

"No," he said hoarsely. He pulled her roughly against him and said, "Your father gave you to me and you will submit."

He swooped down to claim her mouth, and the line between reality and fantasy blurred. She pushed lightly against his chest with both of her hands and struggled just enough to stir his excitement to a level he'd never experienced before.

Before he lost all control and took her right there on Dominic's patio, Rachid broke off the kiss and closed a hand around one of her wrists. "Come," he said and dragged her behind him down the stairs toward the airfield.

"Where are you taking me?" she asked, her voice rising with distress. A quick look back confirmed that her eyes were dancing with an excitement that belied her words.

He stopped walking and pulled her into his arms again, growling into one of her ears, "Somewhere private where I can enjoy you."

She pulled away from him, attempting to free the wrist he still held firmly in one hand. "You'll never get away with this!" she said, her small chest heaving.

Effortlessly, he picked her up and swung her over one of his shoulders. She kicked her legs and hit his back—although there was no sting to either of those flails. "You will learn to obey me, woman."

"Never," she hissed.

Head high, he carried her that way to his private plane. Per his earlier instructions, it had been readied and the pilot was near the open hatch. The expression on the pilot's face was priceless. "Your Highness?" he asked in a worried tone.

Rachid issued his order harshly. "Tell no one of our extra guest. Do you understand?"

When the pilot hesitated, Rachid put Zhang down beside him and loomed over the man, repeating himself between gritted teeth. "Do you understand?"

"Yes, Your Highness. Of course."

Before looking away, Rachid added, "And I will require absolute privacy in the main cabin. Don't open that door, no matter what you hear."

"Of course," the man said nervously.

Once inside the plane, Rachid led Zhang to an area where two seats faced each other. He deposited her in one of them and sat in the other, positioned directly across from her. They both waited until the pilot had closed the hatch to speak.

Zhang laughed into her hand. "I think he really believes that you're kidnapping me."

The corners of Rachid's eyes crinkled with humor, but instead of breaking role with her he said, "Remove your underclothing before you secure your seatbelt."

Her head tipped to the side in question.

He secured himself in his seat and folded his arms across his chest. "Do as I say. We have a six-hour flight, plenty of time to start your education."

"My education?" she asked, her eyes widening.

"Don't make me hunt down a way to tape your mouth shut. Do not question me, woman. Now, take it off."

Zhang held his eyes for a long moment, then stood and raised the hem of her already short dress. She slid her fingers beneath the sides of her silk panties and slid the tiny material down her legs and over her high heels, dropping them on the floor between them.

His mouth dried in anticipation.

"Sit," he croaked.

She did, her eyes never leaving his. The click of her seatbelt echoed in the quiet plane cabin, quickly followed by the roar of the engine starting up.

"Adjust your dress so that I can see you."

Flushing, she did.

"Touch yourself," he instructed.

She didn't move.

"You don't have a choice," he added and waited. Her inexperience in this area was clear. "Have you ever pleasured yourself?"

The pink on her cheeks deepened and she looked away. Sexy and adorable. Adventurous and vulnerable. His attraction to her intensified. "There are no secrets between master and slave. Tell me."

In the safety of the game, she admitted, "I have, but it's not something I've ever shared with someone."

The hint of yearning in her voice spoke to Rachid louder than her words. She was a woman who controlled every aspect of her life and the lives of many around her. She wanted to step outside of that for a night and be free, and he knew that feeling all too well. Perhaps he couldn't give her forever, but he could give her the fantasy she craved. Keeping his voice harsh he said, "Your comfort is of no importance to me. I wish to see you bring yourself pleasure. I will see your juices on your own hand and an orgasm in your eyes."

She shook her head slightly. "I don't think I can. Not with you watching."

He studied her for a moment, then said, "You must because tonight you belong to me."

As the plane left the ground, Zhang lifted her dress with one hand and reached downward with her other. Her eyes held his as she slipped a finger inside her folds. Her movements were awkward at first, almost tentative, until she found a rhythm and closed her eyes.

"That's it, Zhang," he said huskily. "Let go and enjoy."

Faster and faster, her delicate hand rubbed her most sensitive spot, as she scooted forward in the seat to reach herself better. Rachid shifted as he swelled uncomfortably in his pants, but this was not about him, it was about the amazing woman before him and he didn't want to miss a second of it.

Her back arched and she flung her head back.

Nipples erect and reaching, yearning for a touch Rachid would deny for now, Zhang ran her other hand down one of her taunt thighs, rubbing at her own skin hungrily. Her lips parted as her breathing became more ragged.

"Slide your arms out of your straps and ease the top of your dress down." She obeyed, exposing the sheer perfection of her small breasts. He imagined how perfectly they would fill his mouth, how soft they would feel against his skin.

"Now, lick your thumb," he commanded softly. "Take it into your mouth as you would me. In and out, nice and slow. That's it. Take it deep. Circle it with your tongue. Can you imagine my taste? Do you feel your own hot breath on your hand, a sweetness that I will soon feel? Wet that finger well." Watching her suckle on herself was an exquisite torture. He was throbbing in his pants and eager to replace her thumb with his manhood, but patience intensified pleasure. And Zhang was a pleasure he was not going to rush.

When he could take no more, he ordered, "Now, circle the tip of your breast—imagine my tongue there, wet and worshipping. Cup yourself as I would. Enjoy the feel of your own skin, your own softness."

She did as he commanded, and a rose-pink flush spread across her chest.

He said, "You are so wet and ready for me, Zhang. Slip one of your fingers inside yourself. Take it out slowly and then bury it within yourself as you imagine that I would bury myself in you. In and out. Deeper and faster. Feel your own want, your own need." She did and moaned with pleasure. "Open your eyes."

When she did, her hot gaze locked to his. Her mouth opened slightly and her tongue flicked across her lips as if seeking his kiss. His kept his arms folded across his chest, not attempting to disguise the desire in his own face.

Their journey together was only beginning.

"Come for me, Zhang," he whispered.

Without looking away, she increased the tempo of her hand movement and gasped. Another moan escaped her, her stomach tightened and quivered, and she shook as waves of pleasure rocked her slight form.

She slumped into the seat with a shaky breath and withdrew her hand.

"Now," he said with a wicked smile, "you pleasure me. Come here," he demanded softly.

Dress still half on, still humming from the pleasure he'd led her to, Zhang surged out of the seat. Rachid was every bit as amazing as she had imagined and more, so much more. They didn't know each other in the way that many couples did, but on another level she felt that he understood her as no man had before.

Understood and accepted.

He didn't make any promises and she wouldn't have believed him if he had. Nothing this excruciatingly perfect could survive the test of reality. Perhaps that was part of what made the entire experience that much more poignant, knowing that it would soon be nothing more than a memory.

But oh, what a memory.

Rachid stood and looked down at her like some conquering warrior. He shed his jacket but left the rest of his clothing on. "You will undress me."

She stepped forward and reached for the buttons of his shirt, but he stilled her hands with his. "Start with my shoes," he commanded.

A shiver of excitement sliced through Zhang as she bent before him and began to untie his shoes. There was something incredibly sexy about performing the humbling task. When both of his feet were bare, she once again stood proudly before him and awaited his instruction.

"Now my belt," he said, his voice thick with passion.

Zhang fumbled at first when she tried to maintain eye contact while performing the deed, and she had to look down to complete the task. When she reached for the button at the top of his trousers, he said, "Did I tell you to do that?"

She stopped and choked on a laugh. "No."

Rachid was certainly enjoying his role.

She looked up into his eyes and amusement left her as the desire in his eyes relit the heat between her thighs. Tonight was a game, and yet there was a thread of something intensely powerful and meaningful woven through it.

"Remove your dress—slowly."

She reached behind herself and unzipped the dress slowly. Hoping each move was as exciting for him as it was for her, she eased the dress over her small hips and stepped out of it when it hit the floor. She slipped her shoes off.

"I didn't—"

She lifted her chin. "You will never fully control me."

A corner of his mouth curled at the challenge. "The

pleasure will be in trying to." He placed his hands on his hips and ordered, "When you remove my pants and shirt, rub those incredible nipples against me—on my back, my chest, and then against my legs when you are finished and kneeling at my feet."

She stepped closer, pulled his shirt out of his pants and began to unbutton the material that stood between her and the intimate caress they both anticipated. Pushing his shirt open, she ran her hands up his muscled chest and brushed her eager mounds along the same path.

Her reward was his sharp intake of breath. He might have been issuing the commands, but he was also surrendering himself to the experience. His excitement surged against her bare leg and a responding eagerness spread through Zhang.

She dropped his shirt and circled behind him, rubbing her bare chest against him as she went. Loving the heat of him, the strength of him. Hers for the taking.

She ran her tongue lightly across the base of his spine and gloried in the shiver she felt rock through him. Moving around him, she teased his stomach with the heat of her breath, undid his pants and slid his boxer shorts down along with his formal wear.

Kneeling before him, she sat back on her feet and savored the view of him standing fully erect above her. When she made no move to touch him further, a line of concern creased his forehead. "Zhang?"

She gave him what she hoped was her most reluctantly obedient look.

Although his expression was stern, his words melted her heart. "Don't do anything you don't enjoy."

Had she been the type who was moved easily to tears, she would have spilled a tear or two at his concern for her. Instead, she cocked her head to the side and said, "I'm merely awaiting your instructions."

His shudder of excitement was visible.

"Take me in your mouth, Zhang. Feel what you do to me. Taste my desire for you. Learn how to make me forget everything but you."

For one night, the voice in her head reminded.

One night will be enough.

It has to be.

With renewed resolve, Zhang leaned forward and took his large member into her mouth. Instinct guided her through her inexperience. She sucked and licked, paying attention to which moves made him tense and jut against her mouth.

Somewhere along the way, it stopped being about pleasing him and became about them. His need for her. Her need for him. He was both in control of the situation and completely at her mercy at the same time, and she found the experience uniquely intense.

Every touch, every wet lick sent him closer to the edge. Her hands experimented and found the caresses that changed his breathing and had him moaning helplessly for more.

He tightened in her mouth and he looked down at her, those black eyes hot and wild. Both of his hands came down to hold her head as he spilled into her mouth and she tasted him joyfully.

Mine.

My sexy sheikh.

She pulled back and rested her face against his shuddering stomach. He reached down, lifted her into his arms and carried her across the cabin. He opened a small door in the rear of the plane, revealing a small bed. With a flip of his hand, he threw the blanket back and eased her beneath it, quickly sliding in beside her.

Tucked against his side beneath the blankets, Zhang studied the strong lines of Rachid's face. She ran a hand over the slight hair of his chest and said, "I'm too tired to pretend I don't love this."

He kissed her forehead, closed his eyes and smiled. "Good, because we have to save some energy for the desert castle. I didn't order it decorated with silk pillows for nothing."

Zhang raised her head and looked down at him until he

opened his eyes. "You did that for me?"

Amusement transformed his face and made him look years younger. "An argument could be made that I did it for myself."

Zhang's eyes blurred with emotion. "I will never forget this, Rachid."

He hugged her to him and tried to lighten the mood with a joke. "I should hope not." When she opened her mouth to say more, he silenced her with a deep kiss. He didn't stop until excitement once again burned within her again and she squirmed against his side. Then he said, "Sleep, Zhang. We have a few more hours of travel and then a half day left of your fantasy."

How is a half of a day ever going to be enough?

Just before she succumbed to slumber, a voice tickled her consciousness.

You didn't ask for forever, Zhang. There is a much steeper price for that.

Anything, she answered in a fervent whisper. *I'd do anything.*

With that, she broke one of her own fundamental beliefs: Never offer more than you are willing to give.

Chapter Five

An hour later, tucked against her lover's side, enjoying the warmth of Rachid's bare skin against hers, Zhang wasn't about to move. She didn't want to think about yesterday or tomorrow. She breathed in the slight scent of the man holding her and closed her eyes again.

Rachid absently rubbed her shoulder as if he were savoring the moment along with her. "Zhang?" he asked softly.

She didn't respond.

His chest rumbled with relaxed humor. "I know you're awake."

She opened one eye and peered at him. "I might not have been."

He smiled down at her and gently kissed her lips. "Do you really wish to sleep through half of your fantasy?"

His tenderness confused her, pulled at her emotions. "When I told you about it I never expected you to go along with it."

He ran a finger lightly down her back and said, "We have more in common than you know."

She pulled back a bit so she could see his face and asked smartly, "You also fantasize about desert sheikhs?"

His chest rumbled again, and her reward was a light reprimand of hand to rump beneath the sheets. "No, but I understand what it's like to want to step outside your life for a day."

His serious response stilled her teasing. She laid a hand on his chest and said, "We don't know each other, but... "

He nodded and finished her sentence: "But somehow we do."

"Yes," was all she could say.

"Today is also a gift for me," he said.

She held her breath as he gave of himself in a way she'd never expected.

"I often feel like I am two men—and neither of them the one I wanted to be. Outside of Najriad I am a foreigner. It doesn't matter how well I speak English or blend in. Perhaps because of my title or the state of the world, I don't know the precise reason, but I am always a stranger even within countries where I have lived for a decade."

"And when you go home?" Zhang knew what he was going to say even before he spoke.

"It's worse. I'm still an outsider because I have spent so much time away. I don't understand half of the jokes. I'm not even sure I want to. Proximus is hugely successful, and soon I will take my father's place as King of Najriad. Both are an honor I should rejoice about."

"I understand," Zhang said softly.

He gave her a gentle smile. "I believe you do. I have never met a woman like you, Zhang. If the consequences were mine alone to bear, I would..."

"I know," she said, cutting off something she was sure she couldn't bear to hear, and laid her head on his chest. She couldn't choose him over the people she employed back in China. Her schedule was tight with meetings, projects and commitments. She sighed and hugged him. "I can't either. My business keeps me tied to China. I love my country. There is a piece of me that rejoices each time I smell the familiar scent of peach blossoms. How can I love my country so deeply and still feel that I don't belong there? Is it possible to have many houses and not a home?"

He didn't provide an answer to her question, but she hadn't expected him to.

He said, "Come, we should get dressed. We will arrive in Najriad soon."

Zhang closed her eyes instead and said, "Just a few more

minutes."

He tapped her rump lightly again and said, "You are not a very obedient sex slave."

She murmured, "I'll work on that when we land."

His hand settled possessively on her bare rump, easing her hips intimately forward to rub her moist center on one his thighs. "I wish we had time to work on it now... however, in a few moments the pilot will announce our descent." He kissed her deeply. "And I have no intention of rushing with you."

Zhang laughed up into his eyes. "Yes, master." As she spoke, she slid her hand beneath the sheet and gave his already erect member a quick caress. "We must wait." With that she broke contact and rolled out of bed.

In all his naked splendor, he joined her near the door of the small bedroom with a speed she hadn't expected from a relaxed Rachid. "Are you always so brave?" he asked, leaning over her.

Playfully, she opened the door behind her and backed out of the room with a smile on her face. "You should see me when I'm angry."

"I hope I never do," he said softly, following her to where they had both left their clothing. "Although I may enjoy the experience."

"If you survive it," she answered lightly.

Fantasy and friendship blended in a shared smile while they gathered their clothing. Moments later, dressed, Zhang took a seat near one of the windows and prepared for the landing. The dark desert below was illuminated by the lights of the airfield they circled. She said, "I feel like a teenager sneaking around in the middle of the night, hoping we don't get caught."

Rachid claimed the seat beside her and secured himself in. "It's imperative that no one discovers you're here. There are those who would..."

She took his hand and squeezed it. "Trust me, you don't have to explain. No one can ever know about this."

"I have to be in Nilon, the capital city, by tomorrow

evening. If we fly you out around eleven, you should be back on Isola Santos by evening. Will that work for you?"

Who knew heaven came with an itinerary?

Odd as it was to step outside their passion and define the parameters of their time together, it was also somehow reassuring. They were free to be as honest and intense as they wanted to be without real risk—safe in the knowledge that, although exciting, this would change nothing.

The lush gardens of the Salnyra Oasis buffered the ancient castle from the harshness of the surrounding desert. It was easy to imagine the luxurious comfort it had once provided weary travelers in the past. A reprieve sustained by the teasing generosity of an underground river that kept its precious, life-giving waters otherwise hidden.

The castle itself proudly displayed the scars of time. Outside of the modern lighting visible through the windows, it looked as it probably had for centuries. A place outside of time. The perfect place to escape to.

A lone man dressed in a long white robe and matching white keffiyeh met them on the airfield. Rachid issued a few curt instructions in Arabic. The man said something quickly, then bowed and disappeared back into the castle.

Rachid's expression softened when he looked down at Zhang and said, "Come, everything is prepared."

But am I? Zhang thought nervously.

When you're going to do something outrageous and spontaneous, you really shouldn't give yourself time to think about it. *We've already been intimate. What am I afraid of?*

He led her down immaculate but aged hallways to two ornate wooden doors. Releasing her hand, he opened the doors, and Zhang gasped at what his move revealed.

In every direction, tapestries hung from the center of the tall ceiling and cascaded down the walls, creating the illusion of being inside a lavish tent. The room was lit softly by candles that were scattered on small tables around the room. The entire floor was covered with a ridiculous number of richly colored pillows.

Okay, finally reality trumped fantasy.

Zhang entered the room in wonder, allowing herself time to appreciate the care that had gone into creating this setting. She turned to Rachid and said, "I can't believe you did all of this for me."

He stood beside her, his hand resting possessively at the base of her spine, and said, "Surely you have spent time with men of wealth and influence before."

Zhang looked up him and said, "Yes, but often they're so concerned with showing me what they have that they don't listen to what I need." She laid a grateful hand on one of his shoulders. "No one has ever gone this far to please me."

"Then you've been with the wrong men."

"Man," Zhang corrected quietly.

Rachid smiled, "Is it wrong that I'm pleased to hear that?"

She smiled back. "A little."

He pulled her against him and rubbed her back absently. "Just before we entered the castle, a small line of worry appeared right here." He lightly touched the middle of her forehead with one finger. "You don't owe me anything, Zhang. If this isn't what you want, the plane is likely already refueled. Say the word and you're free."

Her breath caught in her throat. Beneath the wildness of the evening there was something much more tempting, and it needed to be denied or it would threaten the safety of their deal. No tomorrows, just tonight. She said, "What a disappointing speech for a master to give his slave."

He grabbed her by both arms and gave her a delicious smile. "Disappointing? Well, I'll have to see what I can do about that."

Resuming her earlier role, Zhang flung her head to the side and said, "You can do whatever you want to my body, but I will never submit to you."

He pulled her closer, rubbing her arched body against his growing excitement. "Whatever I want. I like that sound of that."

When he leaned down to kiss her, she spun her face away. His firm hand took her chin and turned it back, forcing her to look up at him. "Open your mouth for me, Zhang."

Her lips parted even as she considered fighting him. His mouth came down heavily on hers, plundering her mouth, taking what she might have given willingly. His hands moved to the back of her dress and slid the zipper down. Without breaking contact, he eased the dress over her small hips and dropped it onto the floor.

He straightened and took a step back.

Zhang was too flustered from his kiss to do more than stare at him wordlessly.

He ran a finger from the base of her neck down the curve of her breast and over her flat stomach. "I hate to cover you up again, but I bought this for you." He moved to retrieve a rectangular box from one of the tables. "Put this on," he instructed and placed the box in her shaking hands.

Zhang placed the box on a nearby pile of pillows and opened it. A small pair of shimmering royal-blue shorts were paired with a floor-length sheer-white jacket that revealed as much as it pretended to conceal. She slipped the shorts on hastily and shivered with excitement as she secured the jacket with its one button.

Rachid took her by one hand and spun her before him. "You'll do."

Her reaction was instant and strong, her shoulders straightened with pride. *Oh, the things I would say if I wasn't pretending to be afraid.*

He laughed down at her. Taking her by one arm, he led her to one particularly lush pile of pillows. He turned on a small radio and a sensual tune filled the room. Then he settled himself down on the pillows and folded his arms across his chest. "You will dance for me."

49

Her stomach sank. *Fantasy or no fantasy, that's not going to happen.*

Zhang said, "No, I don't do that."

He had that pleased smile on his face again. "You mean, you've never danced for a man before?"

She crossed her arms protectively across her chest. "Exactly, and there are certain things that I'm not comfortable with even if this isn't real."

He rubbed his chin thoughtfully. "I am going to enjoy teaching you how to please a man."

"You can try, but there is nothing about how I dance that will do that."

Rachid stood and stepped toward her. "Silence, slave, or you will be punished."

Zhang's eyebrows lifted in surprise. "That wasn't part of our agreement. What kind of punishment?"

For just a heartbeat, Rachid maintained a serious face, then he burst into laughter and said, "I have no idea. I didn't order props for that contingency. Now, do me a favor and go back to looking scared."

Zhang joined in the laughter for a moment, filling with a joy she'd thought herself incapable of. Then she schooled her features and attempted a pleading tone. "Please don't hurt me."

With one last chuckle, he said harshly, "I will do as I please with you. Now, no more talking." He circled her as if inspecting a possible purchase. "Every woman can dance, just as every woman can orgasm—all it requires is the right partner." He kissed her neck from behind and said, "Dancing can be just as intimate, if you allow it to be."

Okay, I'm in. Her hands fell to her sides in submission.

"I don't mind educating you in this, my lovely slave. Pleasing me is your goal, but that doesn't mean that your own pleasure cannot be found along the way." He took a step back and said, "Move the parts of your body that you would have my lips taste. Tempt me and I will reward you well."

Both turned on and feeling a bit foolish, Zhang moved one

hand playfully. He lifted her hand and kissed her knuckles and moved those delicious lips down her fingers and back up to nip gently at the inside of her wrist.

Zhang raised both of her arms above her head and waved her hands in what she considered a poor imitation of what she had seen dancers in the movies do. Rachid took both of her hands in his, held her hands above her and took his time running his lips ever so sensuously down the length of one and then up the length of the other.

He held her eyes and waited

She wiggled one shoulder. His hands slid down her arms and he pushed the collar of her jacket aside so he could kiss what she'd tempted him with. Zhang rolled her head to one side and the movement drew his lips to the curve of her neck. She raised her chin and his worshipping mouth followed that path.

Turning before him, she moved her other shoulder. Instantly his hands came around from behind her and unbuttoned the jacket, easing it off her and letting it drop to the floor. His lips moved across her back to the shoulder she'd wiggled. She arched her back slightly and he caressed her spine and the curve of her back.

Zhang turned again and lifted one foot from the floor. Rachid dropped to his knees and held her foot in one of his hands. He kissed the arch of her foot, the inside of her ankle. He licked the inside of her calf with his hot tongue, then let her foot fall gently back to the floor. He took a moment to appreciate her only remaining wisp of clothing, then slid it down her legs.

Completely exposed again, Zhang didn't move. Rachid ran a hand warmly up her other leg and lifted it. For a moment Zhang thought he was going to kiss her other foot, but instead he draped her now-shaking leg over one of his shoulders and said, "All good dancing involves the hips."

Oh, God.

Zhang shifted her hips from side to side and then waited.

Cupping her rear from behind with one hand, Rachid brought Zhang to his mouth. His tongue lapped and parted her.

When he paused, Zhang moved her hips slightly and was rewarded with an increase in the speed of his intimate caress. She brought one hand down to steady herself as he teased and entered her, his tongue withdrawing only to circle her pulsing nub.

He paused again and she instinctively arched for him.

He eased her leg back onto the floor and stood again.

"Dance for me, Zhang. Imagine my lips on each part that you move for me, and each temptation will be rewarded. Use your body to show me what you like."

Suddenly it was difficult to choose which appendage to move first. She wanted his kisses everywhere. The music added a rhythm to her movements. She offered him her arms, her shoulders, her back. She arched her chest and shimmied her small endowments with an enthusiasm she'd never imagined she could. The beat moved her feet, but desire moved her hips. She spun before him, exposing her neck again and again to him.

Looking playfully at him over one shoulder, she wiggled her behind and a grin broke out across his face. He was beside her in a flash, his hot lips making good on their earlier promise. He eased her down onto the pillows to allow himself better access. The mountain gave way beneath them and they rolled together, ending in a tangle on yet another layer of pillows. His clothing denied her the pleasure that would have come from the contact of skin on skin.

She straddled him and said, "You have far too much clothing on."

He rolled her beneath him and shed his clothing quickly. When he settled himself on top of her, his excitement full and ready for her, he said, "Didn't I warn you about talking?"

She nodded.

He donned a condom with expertise and spread her legs wider. He lifted her hips and placed a pillow beneath them, positioning her perfectly for him to enter her with ease. And he did, but only with his tip. He entered, then retreated and rubbed against her throbbing folds. When she thought she could take no more, he entered her in one bold thrust that sent heavenly heat rushing through her. When she would have started to move with him, he withdrew again and she almost sobbed.

"If you must speak, then you must beg. Tell me what you want."

His lips hovered over hers.

His manhood hovered over her ready center.

Zhang's hands closed hungrily on Rachid's back. "I want you inside me. Now."

He licked her bottom lip. "Beg." His tip teased her folds.

Zhang's eyes locked with Rachid's, all pride or pretense falling away. "Please," she begged urgently. "Please."

He entered her fully, his hands holding her hips firmly. Just when she thought it couldn't get better than his forceful thrusts, he adjusted her again and hit a spot that sent her into mindless abandon.

The waves ebbed, but the pleasure didn't. He rolled so she was straddling him again, with him still inside her. He moved her hips until she met him thrust for thrust. Kneeling gave her the freedom to find her own pleasure while giving him his. She felt his release and bent to kiss him while she enjoyed a second round of ecstasy.

She slumped onto him. When she would have said something, he put a finger to her lips and said, "Don't speak, I don't have the energy yet to punish you again."

She smiled against his finger and nodded.

Their breathing slowed and she fell asleep on top of him.

The next few hours passed with a combination of periodic naps, gentle exploration and slow pleasuring. Pretense was forgotten and they were simply two people who had stepped outside of their regular lives and tasted heaven.

A knock on the suite door abruptly brought them back to reality. Rachid stood quickly, pulled on the pants of his tux and answered the door shirtless, leaving Zhang buried in a pile of pillows. He threw the door open and bellowed in Arabic, "I told you not disturb me."

A traditionally dressed older man Rachid had yet to learn the name of said quickly, "My apologies, Your Highness, but your father and brother are in the library and wish to speak to you."

With that, fantasy time shattered like a glass dropped on a tile floor.

"Tell them I will be with them in five minutes."

The man bowed slightly and closed the door after saying, "As you wish, Your Highness."

Rachid turned to see Zhang standing in the middle of the room wrapped in one of the tapestries. "Rachid?"

"Get dressed, Zhang." No use trying to sneak her out—his father knew she was here. There was no other explanation for why he would come to the oasis when they'd already made plans to meet at his palace later that day.

The castle staff must have called him last night.

And why not? They have no allegiance to me.

Zhang stepped forward. "What is it? What happened?"

In frustration, Rachid snapped, "Do as I say! Get dressed. I'll return as soon as I can."

Zhang searched his expression and apparently didn't like what she saw. She said, "There's no way that I'm going to wait here quietly unless you tell me what's going on."

Rachid was too busy tucking his shirt into his pants and hunting down his shoes to answer. If Ghalil was with his father, things were going to get worse before they got better. A quick check in the mirror made him groan.

I look like I spent the night doing... exactly what I was doing.

Damn.

He tried to tame his wild hair but gave up. It was more important not to keep his father waiting.

I should have anticipated this possibility.

His father would never understand a woman like Zhang.

With any luck, her identity wasn't known. The faster he got her out of the country, the safer it would be for her. Instinctively, he took a key off a small table near the door.

She hadn't moved.

He groaned. "You need to get dressed and be ready to leave by the time I return." She opened her mouth to say something, but he cut her off and said, "My father is here." With that, he closed the door behind him and locked it.

The door rattled as Zhang tested it.

Rattled louder as she retested it.

A thud that might have come from an angry open hand smacking against the door revealed her feelings about being detained. As did the Chinese curses that followed him down the hallway: "Open this door, Rachid."

A small smile pursed his lips. Each castle door had been built as a last line of defense for a family to hide behind if the castle were ever invaded and should be able to contain one petite, furious Zhang.

The door rattled again.

Unfortunately, he didn't have the luxury of time to watch her test his theory. He navigated the long hallways with purposeful haste. When he entered the library he walked directly to his father, gave a slight bow of deference and said, "Father." Despite the look of anger he saw on his younger brother's face, he greeted him warmly: "Ghalil."

Dressed in a simple, traditional white thobe, white keffiyeh and black agal, the older man was an intimidating figure. His voice was soft, but a man like Amir didn't require volume to make his displeasure known. With his hands clasped behind his back, he said, "I received a rather disturbing phone call this morning."

Rachid bowed his head in acknowledgement. "You shouldn't have been contacted, Father. It's a personal matter."

"I would say kidnapping is a family concern," his father countered calmly.

"Kidnapping?" Rachid thought back to the role-playing he

and Zhang had enacted in front of the pilot the night before. *We were that convincing?* He didn't hide the small smile the memory elicited. *Seriously? That's why the staff involved my father?* "Let me assure you..."

Ghalil interrupted, "It's as I said, Father. He doesn't care how this may endanger all of us. He thinks only of himself and satisfying his immoral lifestyle."

How do you really feel, Ghalil? Rachid thought sarcastically. His younger brother's opinion wasn't a surprise or a concern at the moment, but the displeasure on his father's face was. "None of this will endanger anyone. She came with me willingly and she leaves this morning."

Ghalil continued his verbal assault and went nose to nose with his brother. "You think we care if she was willing? Victim or woman of no virtue, it matters not. She's here and evidence that you're not fit to rule."

A hot fury seared through Rachid. His hands clenched at his sides. "Speak of me as you wish, Brother, but you will not mention her again."

"I will do as I —" Ghalil started, pulling a fist back aggressively.

Rachid didn't raise a hand to defend himself. He stood, holding his brother's eyes, neither engaging nor backing down.

"Enough!" Amir roared before contact was made. "Control yourself, Ghalil."

Ghalil's hands fell to his sides. The young man spun on his heel and addressed his father angrily. "Me? He makes a mockery of his title and you correct me?"

The stern lines on Amir's face deepened. His words were spoken softly but held a warning. "You forget your place, Son—and Rachid's."

Neither son needed to have that reprimand translated. Amir was reminding Ghalil that Rachid would soon become king. Angry red stained the younger brother's cheeks. Rachid felt sympathy for him and a sadness as the chasm between them widened.

Amir ordered quietly, "Sit down, Ghalil. This conversation is between Rachid and me."

Visibly shaking with anger, Ghalil did as his father asked. He took a seat nearby, across from his brother, with the bottom of his feet facing Rachid in an age-old insult: *You are beneath my feet.*

The move only saddened Rachid more. A brother was a gift. Would his always be an angry stranger? While he was amassing his fortune, Rachid hadn't had time to get to know Ghalil. Only now did he admit to himself that he'd hoped his return would change that.

When Rachid met his father's eyes again, he was surprised to see real concern there. "You take my title in a few months. There is no time for this foolishness. You must win the favor of the people, or you'll have to earn it with your fist. If word spreads of your actions last night, it will be easy to say that you don't care about the real dangers facing us from our neighbors. You need to be seen addressing these attacks, not partying with your American friends and using our castles like brothels. The welfare of the family must come first. What were you thinking, Rachid?"

A man like his father would never understand how last night had been about so much more than sex. He considered it irresponsible and selfish. Worse, he was right. *I gave my needs priority over the safety of those I love.* Real shame settled heavily on his heart. "I wasn't thinking, Father. I'm sorry."

His father approached him and laid a hand on his arm. "You've always done what I have asked of you. And you've done it well, son. You'll succeed here, but it will not be easy." He dropped his hand and said, "Get this woman out of the country immediately and speak to no one of this."

He wasn't the weak link in the room. Rachid looked over his shoulder at his brother, who stood in response to the unspoken question. Ghalil sneered, "Unlike you, Rachid, I would never do anything to endanger Najriad. My silence will be because it's best for our people and our family, not for you."

Am I not family? Rachid thought sadly, but said nothing.

A knock on the door interrupted his thoughts. The old servant entered, bowed slightly and directed his announcement to the man who held his loyalty. "A thousand apologies, Your Excellence, but the royal advisor has landed on the airfield. I thought you should know."

King Amir's eyebrows met in question, but he merely said, "Bring him here."

"As you wish, Your Excellence."

Basir? Here? And Father didn't know he was coming? That can't be good.

Dressed in a gold-embroidered blue thobe and keffiyeh, the royal advisor swept into the room. His white hair and weathered skin were a testament to the number of years he had loyally served the Hantan family. If Rachid succeeded in ascending to king, his would be the third generation to trust this man's sage advice.

He bowed before his king briefly and said, "I have come with a matter of great importance."

Amir greeted the man with a familiar a hug. "What has happened, Basir?"

The older man held out an international English newspaper and said, "I have been fielding phone calls since this photo hit the news this morning." His father studied the paper for a moment, then handed it to Rachid.

There, in all of its front-page glory, was a photo of him carrying a flailing Zhang up the steps of his private plane. The headline read, NAJRIAD PRINCE KIDNAPS CHINESE BILLIONAIRESS FROM CORISI WEDDING. CHINA DEMANDS HER IMMEDIATE RETURN.

Rachid skimmed the article, which was full of lies from "sources." The validity of the picture, however, could not be denied. *Shit.*

Ghalil peered over Rachid's arm and jeered, "Do you still

think your actions harm no one?"

Rachid looked at him quickly. *No, he couldn't have. He wouldn't have. Yes, they had their differences, but his brother wouldn't lower himself to this.*

Amir directed his question to his advisor. "You've spoken with the Chinese minister of foreign affairs?"

Basir nodded. "And the Chinese ambassador—twice this morning. They're furious, but they don't exactly want her back."

Amir nodded with understanding.

Rachid demanded, "Then what do they want?"

The older man turned to Rachid and said, "They'd like to see you publicly, severely punished or..."

Or had to be better.

". . . or they want the two of you to marry immediately."

Rachid swayed back on to his heels. *Not the "or" I was hoping for.*

Amir straightened and roared. "My son will not marry some tramp to appease China. If anyone should be punished, it should be her. Obviously she orchestrated this. How else would the news have such a perfect photo of the folly? Tell the papers she was willing and that there will be no punishment for my son. Let her deal with the consequences of her choices."

Basir said, "The minister won't be happy."

The king replied, "No one is happy about this, but it's done. I will not speak further of this foolishness." He walked to the window and looked out, dismissing all behind him without a word.

Rachid stepped forward and said, "Father, I can't let you do that."

His father turned slowly. His features stern. "It is done, Rachid."

Rachid went to his father's side. "No, Father, it is not."

Amir studied Rachid for a moment. "This woman is important enough that you challenge me, son?"

Rachid didn't look away. "Father, it is with the greatest

respect that I tell you that I cannot go along with your plan. She doesn't deserve to be treated this way." As he spoke, his resolve grew. "I promised her that nothing would come from our time together."

Those wise old eyes narrowed slightly at the unexpected steel in his son's voice. "You're willing to marry the woman? Her honor is worth your freedom?"

An image of Zhang tucked into his side, smiling shyly up at him with complete trust, made the answer easy. "Yes," Rachid said with conviction and without hesitation.

Ghalil interjected, "You think you can marry her and the scandal will simply go away? It's not that easy."

Basir countered the young prince's statement. "It may be. Especially if we don't tell anyone that she was willing."

All three men looked at the older advisor in surprise.

He explained, "Rachid, you've done well in business, but people question if you have what it takes to stand up to our enemies. This is a bold move, and not backing down to China will impress many. You saw a woman at a wedding. You took her. In our ancient laws, you haven't broken the law as long as she agrees to marry you within a week. She'll have to be questioned apart from you, however, and she'll need to say that she enters into this marriage of her own free will. If you can convince her to do that, this situation may work in your favor."

Ghalil bristled and asked, "And how will that gain him public approval?"

The advisor smiled. "You're young, Ghalil. You don't know how difficult it is to win the heart of an unwilling woman."

Marriage. It wasn't something he'd considered himself ready for, but he would do it for family, for country, for Zhang.

Rachid straightened his shoulders and said confidently, "Plan the wedding for Saturday. She'll agree to it."

His father rubbed his short beard thoughtfully. "I wish to meet this woman who would be my daughter-in-law, for she has lit a fire in my son that I wasn't sure would ever ignite. Bring her here."

Pride swelled even as he stalled his father. "Give me a few moments with her first, Father. She may need time to warm up to the idea."

Chapter Six

Wrinkled bridesmaid dress or sex-rumpled harem slave costume? What a choice.

Zhang could practically hear the universe laughing as she picked the skintight charcoal dress off the floor and stepped back into it.

Oh, great, I left my underwear on the plane.

Perfect.

She stepped into her high heels and headed to the bathroom to comb her hair. *Makeup would be nice, but really, when a breeze from below is enough to remind you of your folly, will mascara make a difference?*

Pacing the length of the suite, Zhang reviewed the quick change of events that morning. Somehow Rachid's father had found out she was there and was apparently not pleased with the news.

So, he locked me in.

And I would do something about it if —

Oh, yes, I left my cell phone at the wedding with Lil.

This day just keeps getting better and better.

Zhang spun at the sound of a key being turned in the door. She stopped midstep and stared at the man who walked in. From the top of his white keffiyeh —covered head to the hem of his long white thobe, Rachid looked every bit the Arab prince she'd imagined in her fantasies, but nothing in his expression implied he had come to play. He held a large rectangular box in one hand.

I hope his apology comes with panties.

Rachid laid the box on the small table near the door. He walked toward her and she held her breath. Standing only a few inches away from her, he said, "Zhang, things have changed."

She couldn't stop herself from saying, "Yes, they have. You locked me in." She glared at him, angry all over again. "You know all that stuff about not wanting to be in control? That ended when we woke up this morning. I hope you have the plane readied, because I'm leaving—right now."

"No," he said, slowly shaking his head. "You're not."

"Yes, I am," Zhang said firmly, planting her feet slightly apart. "We had a deal. One night. I leave. No one ever knows. That's what you agreed to."

He reached to caress her face, but she pulled back from him angrily. He said, "What we planned doesn't matter anymore." He showed her the newspaper Basir had brought.

Zhang read the headline and sagged in shock. Rachid caught her by the elbows.

Oh, my God.

"What are we going to do?" she asked before she'd thought her question through. There was no *we*, only two separate people who had done something incredibly stupid together. He didn't owe her anything, and that was very likely what he was just about to tell her.

"We prepare for our wedding," he said calmly.

Zhang almost sunk to the floor, but he propped her up again. "I'm sorry," she said. "I thought you just said 'our wedding.' "

A patient smile curled a side of his mouth. "You heard me. I don't love the idea, either, but we don't have much of a choice."

Zhang closed her eyes. *As far as proposals went, his fell pretty flat.*

"It doesn't have to be forever," he added.

Wow, that makes it even more tempting. Opening her eyes again, she tried to focus on what Rachid was saying instead of the growing storm of emotion in her heart.

He continued, "My people are not in favor of divorce, but it does happen. A year from now, we can separate over cultural differences and everyone will understand."

Zhang ripped her arms out of his grasp and said, "I appreciate your very romantic proposal, but I have to decline. I can't marry you, Rachid. I have a business to run. And although this may not look good in the news, it will pass and people will forget about it. We don't have to do anything drastic."

Rachid's expression set in harsh lines. "As we speak, my father is informing the Chinese minister of foreign affairs that we'll be married this coming weekend."

Zhang stood toe-to-toe with him, hands on hips, and said, "That's a problem, because we are not getting married."

Instead of arguing the point, Rachid walked over and picked up the box near the door and handed it to her. "My father would like to you meet you. I suggest you wear this."

Zhang took the box angrily. "Good. I'd like to meet your father so I can tell him what I told you. I'm not marrying anyone."

Rachid tipped her head up with one finger and said softly, "I suggest you don't. My father's word is law. If he decides to execute you for dishonoring our family, even I couldn't stop him. And if you think your government is going to storm in here and save you, you're more naïve than I took you for."

Zhang yanked her chin away from him but held her tongue. She wasn't fool enough to take them on while they were in control of the situation. She could play along just long enough to gain an opportunity to contact her people. Government support was unnecessary. She had a small security force who would give their lives for her. All she had to do was get word to them. Composing her features, Zhang said, "Fine. I'll meet your father and I'll play nice. But it doesn't change anything."

Rachid looked down into her eyes and looked like he wanted to say more, but instead he bowed slightly and went to the door. "I'll tell him you will meet us in thirty minutes."

Zhang nodded once. As she saw him take the key out of his pocket again, she rushed toward the door but was too late to stop him from locking her in again. She threw the box angrily against the door and said, "Even in my fantasy, you didn't lock me in!"

It didn't help her mood that she heard him laugh on the other side of the door.

Oh, that man is going to pay.

Chapter Seven

She didn't want to love the dress, but the simplicity of the long-sleeved gold-leaf gown with a sheer-blue overlay was stunning and feminine without being provocative. The square-toed Jimmy Choo gold flats were a welcome accessory. She would have said that she felt more comfortable in simple black slacks, but she reluctantly admitted to herself that these delicate layers of expensive material made her feel beautiful.

All that and underwear.

What more could a woman ask for?

Rachid had even thought of an outfit for her morning walk of shame home? The idea was both mortifying and touching at the same time.

Zhang heard a key in the door and turned from the mirror. A wave of an emotion she quickly denied rushed through her when she realized that it wasn't Rachid at the door. A tall, thin man in his late sixties and dressed in a long tan thobe stood in the doorway. "Please follow me," he said coldly.

She did. As they walked down the hallway, Zhang asked, "What's your name?"

"Abdal," he answered briskly.

"Have you worked here long?" she asked, keeping up with his quick step.

"I was born here," he answered simply.

"Here in this castle?" she asked, surprised.

"Yes, my father was the caretaker before me."

Small talk didn't come easy to Zhang, but if there was a chance that it might win the trust of the servant, she could appear interested in an old castle. "Parts of it look quite modern." Perhaps modern enough to have a phone—though she knew enough not to ask for one yet.

"It has been in the Hantan family for hundreds of years and each generation has tended to it with great care."

Evidence of what the servant said was everywhere Zhang looked as she followed him. The marble floor of the hallway had been carefully laid to create geometric designs, all of which were intact and shone from a recent polishing. The thick walls of the old fortress were virtually windowless. As they approached the main area of the castle, the temperature cooled to a comfortable level. Zhang commented on a cool breeze that wafted past her, and the servant explained that the wind tower was still fully operational and that often the ancient ways were still the best, especially when one lived in the desert.

He opened two large wooden doors and bowed, backing away. Three men stood when she entered the room. Zhang was instantly struck by how much Rachid looked like his father. The same dark, serious eyes. The same proud nose. Rachid was slightly taller, but otherwise there was no denying his lineage. The other man in the room looked to be about twenty years old. He was built more like the father but had an angry fire in his eyes that made it difficult to appreciate what would otherwise have been an attractive face.

"Come, child, and join us," the father said in a mix of invitation and command.

Zhang stepped forward, refusing to meet Rachid's eyes. If they thought they could intimidate her, they were sadly mistaken. She hadn't gotten as far as she had by backing down or giving in to bursts of emotion. She would eat their food and let them speak their piece. As they relaxed, she would discover a weakness or an opportunity to escape.

Patience is its own strategy.

"You may take a seat near your betrothed," the king said.

Outside of one raised eyebrow, Zhang contained her response to his words. *Betrothed, my ass.*

Rachid held out a chair for her. Zhang grit her teeth but still didn't look up at him. Looking would only loosen her angry tongue. Instead, she met the father's eyes briefly, politely, then looked respectfully down at the table before her.

The king said, "Rachid tells me that you have a successful real estate development business in China."

Zhang once again looked at the older man and simply nodded. The less she said, the better. This wasn't about winning them over or making a point, it was about biding her time.

"You also made some of your money from dealing with spices internationally."

Zhang nodded again.

"It will not be easy for you to leave all of that behind, I think." As he spoke he watched her expression closely. Zhang didn't like that there was a hint of concern in his voice.

I'm not leaving anything behind, she wanted to scream, but she smiled slightly instead. *I am on the first plane out of here as soon as I can get my hands on a phone.*

Beneath the table, Rachid reached out and took one of her hands in his. Zhang pried herself loose and sat straighter in her chair. She didn't need his support, or whatever he thought his touch would give. She was perfectly in control of both herself and the situation.

"I have contacted your parents to ensure them of your safety," the king said.

Zhang's breath caught in her throat. *That must have gone over well.*

He continued, "Of course, they will attend the wedding. I hope you'll inform Rachid of whatever customs you would like us to follow that day to help them feel welcome." He chided gently. "That is, if you speak."

Oh, trust me, I have a lot to say—just nothing that I feel would help this situation.

Breathe.

One perk of being a woman is that men often underestimate you.

Let them think what they wish of me, it'll only help me win in the end.

The king said, "There is much to do. We will travel to Nilon today. Once there, you will stay in the women's quarters until the day of your wedding. My mother speaks English fluently, so she is a natural choice to help you prepare. Regardless of how this started, you join our family on Saturday and will be expected to act accordingly."

An angry fire began to burn within Zhang, but she held it in.

There is only so much of this I can handle.

Rachid spoke, "Zhang is an amazing woman, Father."

The father said, "You certainly picked a beautiful flower for your garden, Rachid."

Zhang's head whipped around to Rachid. The question escaped before she could stop herself. "Garden? As in more than one flower?"

Rachid's eyes held a smile as he asked, "This matters to you?"

Clenching her hands in her lap, Zhang forced a sweet smile. "Not in the slightest."

The king said, "Do not worry, child, a man's first wife always holds a special place in his heart."

That's it.

Zhang stood, laid both hands on the table and snarled, "I'm not worried because there will be no wedding. Rachid can have a hundred wives for all I care. A thousand. You can make whatever plans you'd like and talk about this as much as you want, but it's not going to happen. As soon as I get word to my people, it won't be as easy as locking a door. If you don't release me now, you risk serious consequences and I may not be able to guarantee your safety."

A silence fell over the room.

Rachid's father threw back his head and laughed. Rachid joined him—sending Zhang's blood pressure to volcanic proportions. She grit her teeth and said, "I'm glad you find this amusing. You won't be laughing when my men come."

Rachid stood beside her, his eyes still crinkled with

amusement. "Sit down, Zhang."

Patience be damned.

She spun on him. "I will never marry you. And I don't care if your father is the law of this land. I'd rather be strung up and publicly executed than spend five more minutes listening to either one of you."

She stalked to the door and opened it. A guard blocked her exit. The king spoke to him in Arabic. The man nodded and instructed for Zhang to follow him.

She did, but not before she heard Rachid say something to his father—followed by the deep sound of both men laughing again.

During the walk back to her well-cushioned cell, Zhang decided that the whole taken-by-a-desert-sheikh thing was highly overrated.

No one ever mentioned how much of the time you'd spend wanting to strangle them.

Following Zhang's grand exit, Rachid's father took his seat again, and Rachid followed suit. Ghalil remained standing. He said, "It's obvious that she is completely unsuited for our family."

Rachid tensed. His brother's opinion mattered little compared to his father's.

Amir scratched his short beard and said, "Funny, I was thinking the exact opposite." He smiled at his older son. "I can see what you like about her, Rachid. She has a spirit you don't see in many women."

Ghalil interjected, "Am I the only one who heard her threats?"

Quickly losing patience with his younger brother, Rachid asked, "You fear a woman, Ghalil?"

The young man spat, "That woman will likely kill you in your sleep."

Rachid showed his teeth in what fell short of a smile. "A

circumstance you would benefit from, Brother."

"Enough," Amir said to Rachid. "Save your energy for Zhang. Let us forget all of this nonsense for now and speak of more pressing matters. Rachid, how are your plans to move Proximus' headquarters to Nilon?"

Switching gears quickly, Rachid said, "I needed to increase my liquid assets to do it, but I may have a lead on a deal that would make it possible."

Ghalil sneered. "No wonder you agreed to marry your whore. Everyone knows she's rich."

Rachid surged out of his chair and closed the short distance to Ghalil. Very softly he warned, "Why do you beg for me to do something I will regret? You're my brother. I don't want your blood on my hands."

Ghalil stood tall beneath the threat. "You don't belong here, Rachid. We both know it. And now you've chosen a wife that the people will never accept. It's only a matter of time before you put our family in real danger."

Rachid glanced at his father, but the older man's expression gave nothing away. He looked down at his brother again and some of his anger left him. Ghalil felt justified in his attacks. He saw Rachid as unfit to become king, and some of his arguments were valid. Marrying Zhang was a gamble that could make the situation better—or infinitely worse. Still, it was time to address his brother's growing insolence. "Two things will end a man's life early, Ghalil—overconfidence and talking about another man's woman. Nipping at my ankles will not win you the title you think you deserve, but one day soon it will gain you a swift reprimand."

Ghalil held Rachid's gaze for a minute, then backed down angrily. He clearly had more to say, but he held his tongue.

Their father smiled. "Ah, Rachid, you make me miss my younger years. Go, tame your future wife. You have less than a week to do it, and I suspect you'll need every minute of it."

Rachid returned his smile. "Thank you, Father." He headed for the door.

Amir added, "I can't wait to see the grandchildren you two produce."

Rachid took the parting comment with him into the hallway.

Grandchildren.

That would require a real marriage, and that wasn't what he was planning.

Was it?

Seated beside Rachid in the back of a limo sandwiched in a long caravan of SUVs, Zhang watched the airfield disappear behind them and Nilon rise up before them. *Civilization, thank God. This will soon be over. I just hope I don't go to prison for what I will unleash on this family.*

Rachid whispered in her ear. "Will this silence continue into our marriage? Because I have to admit it's rather pleasant."

Zhang swung around, only to find that the move brought her lips so close to his that she could almost taste his sweet kiss. She licked her lips in memory and kicked herself mentally for the momentary weakness.

He could fight for my freedom, but instead he cowers beside his father.

He's not worthy of me.

Forgetting that for a moment is dangerous.

Between gritted teeth, Zhang said, "You'll regret this, Rachid."

Despite her anger, he touched her cheek and said, "Parts of it I already do. I should never have put you in danger."

"I'm not the one you should worry for now. Look into my eyes and see my intention. I will not be forced into marriage. Remember that nothing is more dangerous than when it's cornered."

Instead of backing down, as she expected, or rising to the challenge as some would have, he took her hand in his and held it on his robed thigh. "One day you will understand that I made the best decision for both of us."

She tugged at her hand but did not succeed in freeing it. While she considered her next move, she said, "Exactly. You made the decision. You live with the consequences."

He turned her hand over in his and rubbed his thumb over her wrist absently, sending unwelcome shivers down Zhang's back. "Do you never tire of fighting, Zhang?" he asked softly.

Yes.

She ripped her hand out of his and snarled, "I haven't even begun to."

He smiled sadly. "Would it help if I told you that you can keep your company? I'll make arrangements to ensure you don't lose it."

Something akin to fear whipped through her. What a cruel twist of fate it would be if one night cost her all the independence she'd fought so hard for. Perhaps it was a fear left over from her humble beginnings, but a part of her had always worried that she could lose everything as quickly as she'd made it. However, even her darkest bouts of insecurity hadn't included the possibility that someone would take it from her. For just a moment, she felt like a young girl again, defending her right to choose her path. "Don't touch me, and don't involve yourself in my business. You have no right to do either." Her eyes glittered with angry tears that she turned away to hide.

He bent and whispered in her ear again. "A husband has many rights, and one of them includes touching. Not that there is an inch of you that I'm not already familiar with."

She stared angrily out the limo window. "You will never be my husband. Enjoy those memories, Rachid, because they are all you'll ever have."

He sat back, seeming to relax into the seat beside her, and said, "We'll see, won't we? I think we've already made progress."

She glared at him over her shoulder.

He folded his arms across his chest and smiled at her shamelessly. "You don't hate me, Zhang. You're afraid to let go

73

and trust me. I can work with that."

"I am not afraid," she denied hotly and turned to study the high-rises that loomed above, blocking out the sun. "I'm not."

This time it was the universe that laughed.

Chapter Eight

The next morning, Rachid was in his private quarters, making a mental plan of how he would woo Zhang. In retrospect, it had been a mistake to mention the possibility of divorcing in a year. Women need a sense of security.

Could a real marriage between them work?

The more he thought about it, the more optimistic he became.

Zhang understood him in a way no woman before her had. She was a phenomenal lover with a sense of humor that would warm his heart when age cooled their ardor. Beautiful, intelligent, accomplished and strong-willed.

Rachid smiled.

A challenge for sure.

A man could spend a lifetime trying to tame a woman like that.

He instantly hardened as he imagined the methods he'd employ. They hadn't used the silk scarves that he'd ordered for the desert castle. He imagined Zhang naked and bound to his bed as he teased her mercilessly until she begged him to take her. Attempting to distract his raging libido, he chose which small cap he would wear beneath his headdress to secure it. He studied his image in the mirror as he folded his keffiyeh and added the black ring around it. *This is who I am—who I need to be.* He shook off the tempting images of a naked Zhang that were challenging his focus. With less than a week to get her to agree to marry him, he'd have to keep a clear head and be more strategic.

He'd start by telling her their marriage would be real. That should bring her some comfort. He could also tell her more about Najriad and his goals for it. Perhaps he'd even ask her for advice. Women liked to feel that their voices were heard. Even as queen, a woman like Zhang would need something outside of their children to occupy her time. He glanced at the folder of research that he'd requested from his security—a summary of Zhang's business holdings. Of course, he would assume control of her company, but she could start a national charity or an educational project.

He wanted her to be happy.

He'd give her wealth without work, a royal title, children and a husband. No, he didn't love her, but he respected her. His strong sense of family and duty would keep him faithful. In return, she'd have to adapt to the ways of his people, but that was a small price to pay for a life any woman would love.

Yes, his mistake had been suggesting that they could divorce. The idea had offended her. A woman like her deserved more. And, if he were honest, one night with Zhang had created a need in him that he didn't think a year of bedding her would lessen. He'd barely slept the night before. He'd lain in his bed craving her as he'd never craved a woman before. He wanted her touch, her kiss, her scent beside him in his bed.

Marriage would give them a lifetime to explore each other.

All he had to do was convince her that she wanted the same thing.

Midmorning, Zhang paced her new gilded cage. If she had been on vacation, she might have appreciated her suite's blend of ancient and modern luxury. She noted the elegance of the room's cream walls, which were accented with gold inlay and a crisp white trim. Although she didn't like to admit it, she'd slept well on the twelve hundred—count bedsheets. The furniture in the bedroom and sitting room could have graced the most luxurious of hotels. Cream couches and other bold-red accent pieces blended well to create an expensive and feminine setting. She could only guess at what the rest of the women's quarters looked like. A female servant who'd come to her room last night to ensure she had everything she needed had told her that the quarters filled an entire wing.

Zhang's rooms were somewhat isolated from the rest of the women's. *Making it less likely for anyone to hear me yell for help.* The large, second-story windows didn't open, and the telephone had been removed. It was a beautiful prison cell, but a prison nonetheless.

As she moved from room to room, the material of her floor-length slate-gray satin dress and its light-pink Erdem lace overlay swished, quietly mocking her choice of attire. The gown was the polar opposite of what she normally chose to wear, but compared to the ultrafeminine collection of clothing Rachid's staff had filled her closet with, it was conservative. Most of the outfits had gold and diamond accents. Some had sequins. Zhang shuddered. *Throw me in the palace dungeon, but please don't dress me in sequins.*

Although the servant had been pleasant enough, her loyalty to the royal family had been obvious. She'd answered Zhang's general questions about the palace, but when Zhang had pushed for specifics her only response had been a polite smile.

When the woman had looked like she was about to leave, Zhang had asked, "What's your name?"

"Abida," the woman answered humbly, not meeting Zhang's eyes.

"Abida, I need a phone. Please. It's important."

The servant merely smiled.

Zhang pressed on urgently, "They are keeping me here against my will. You have to help me."

Another smile, and then the woman said, "If you need anything else, please use the intercom on the wall. It connects to my room." She took out a key.

The room key.

Zhang made a move toward her, but the woman said hastily, "There is a guard outside your door. The lock is only a formality. Please, don't make me call for him."

Zhang offered what she'd thought would tempt any staff member. "I'm a very rich woman. If you help me, you'll never have to work again. I'll set you up in any country you want. I can guarantee your safety here and wherever you decide to go. All I need is five minutes with a phone so I can contact my men."

As the woman opened the door, she said apologetically, "Najriad is my home. You may come to love it, too."

"I won't be here long enough for that to happen," Zhang swore.

The woman bowed her head politely and closed the door behind her. What kind of woman could walk away without helping? She didn't even blink at the offer of money. Loyal staff would hinder Zhang's plans to get to a phone, but they wouldn't stop her. Nothing would.

Every security force had a flaw. She doubted that the palace routinely held women captive. Most likely, the guardsmen were skilled at keeping people out of the palace but lacked experience in containment.

She'd use that weakness to her advantage.

Chapter Nine

An hour later, Abida returned and said, "Prince Rachid would like you to join him for breakfast."

Prince Rachid can kiss my ass, Zhang thought, but she forced a smile. Leaving the room would increase her opportunity to discover a way out. "I'm surprised he didn't deliver the invitation himself."

The woman said, "Men are not allowed inside this wing."

Interesting.

"And yet I have a man with a machine gun standing guard at my door."

"Yes," the woman answered. "The prince thought it was necessary."

I bet he did.

"And the prince gets what the prince wants," Zhang grumbled and followed the woman through the door and down a long white hallway.

"Yes," the woman said, "but he is a generous man, too. He wants you to be comfortable here. Everyone was instructed to keep you safe and as content as possible."

Now, there was a possibly useful bit of information.

"I won't be any level of content as long as I'm kept here against my will. Can't you see that?"

The woman didn't respond. She led Zhang down a main stairway and through another long hallway, where she finally stopped near a door. She raised her hand to knock, but before she did, she said, "You are marrying the prince in a few days. When he becomes king, you will be our queen. I cannot imagine a greater honor." She rapped on the door once softly and opened it, revealing Rachid standing beside a table that had been set for two. The servant bowed and excused herself.

Dressed in the traditional Arab clothing that she was becoming accustomed to seeing him in, Rachid smiled and held out a hand. "You look beautiful this morning."

Zhang ignored his outstretched hand. "Save the compliments. I want access to a phone—now."

Instead of responding, Rachid put a hand on Zhang's lower back and guided her into the room. She hated how her skin warmed and tingled beneath his touch. He held a seat out for her. Zhang considered refusing to sit but decided to choose her battles with care.

"I wasn't sure what you'd like for breakfast, so I had the cook prepare a variety of foods," he referenced the plates of fruits and breads. When she didn't respond, he added, "I can request something else if you'd like."

"I'm not hungry," she said, even as her stomach rumbled and she realized she hadn't eaten anything since the intimate snacks they'd shared at the desert castle.

He took the seat across from her, said, "Suit yourself," and picked up a luscious piece of melon and bit into it. "I'm starving."

Her stomach complained again, loudly this time.

Rachid filled a small plate with fruit and cake-like breads. He put it before Zhang. "Eating won't make me doubt your level of displeasure with me."

Zhang tasted one of the cakes. It melted in her mouth, its deliciousness surely only due to her hunger. Rachid was right— not eating wasn't going to prove anything. She took another heavenly bite.

"Coffee?" he offered.

"Please," she said and marveled at the ridiculousness of their polite exchange. Her mother would cringe at her choice of beverage, but coffee was invigorating and part of the other culture Zhang spent half of her life immersed in. To be successful on a global scale, she'd needed to be as comfortable in the West as she was in the East. And she was, although she sometimes felt it had cost her as much as it had gained her.

Rachid filled her cup and gestured to the cream and sugar. She wondered where the staff was, then decided that he'd probably excused them. You wouldn't want your help to know how much your bride wanted to leave. Although, after meeting Abida, Zhang wasn't sure that anyone would care.

Rachid sat back in his chair and said, "I made a mistake yesterday."

Zhang's eyes flew to his. "Yes, you did."

He continued, "I understand why you're upset."

Hope filled Zhang. *Better late then never.*

He said, "No woman wants to marry a man who talks of divorcing her in year. Your anger is justified. You deserve better than that. I don't have another woman in my life at this time. There's no reason why our marriage can't be real."

Zhang gasped and choked on a crumb. The food lodged in her windpipe, causing her to cough and cough. She took a sip of her coffee and realized too late that, without cream, it was scalding hot.

Rachid handed her a glass of water.

She accepted it angrily and took a fast gulp. As her breathing resumed, she chose the words she'd use to wake her delirious prince up.

He took her hand in his. "I'll take care of your real estate business for you. You'll have every luxury you had before, without any of the worry. You'll finally have the home you were looking for. Here, with me."

Zhang stood, pulling her hand away from his. "You think I'm upset because I can't stay longer? You arrogant ass! The reason why our marriage can't be real is because it's not going to happen." Her chest heaved with anger.

He joined her on one side of the table and slid his hands around her waist, pulling her to press against him. "My proud little Zhang, I can give you everything you've ever wanted."

His excitement hardened between them, sending an answering and unwelcome quiver down her spine. "If you're afraid that this is merely for political reasons, let me assure you that I want to marry you."

Zhang struggled to free herself, but he held her there. The more she struggled, the more excited he became. Despite how angry she was with him and the situation, her own body betrayed her by molding to his form and moistening with hunger for him. *The fantasy is over*, she told herself angrily. Lusting after him would only give him the power he wanted over her. "Take your hands off of me." She readied her knee with intention.

He shifted her upward, removing the risk of her threat. He held her easily with one arm while his hand slid to the front of her dress. He rubbed a thumb over her bodice intimately, easily finding and increasing the evidence of her desire for him. "Are you afraid that you won't be my only wife? Trust me, you're all I'll ever need." He nuzzled her neck. "We could be good together, Zhang."

No, her mind shouted. Instead of fighting him physically, she forced herself to remain still and struck at him with her words. "You're delusional if you think this will change my mind."

His hand cupped one of her breasts. "You will be my wife, Zhang." His mouth descended on hers.

Yes.

No.

How could something so crazy be so tempting to agree to?

His lips claimed hers, hungrily demanding submission from her—a submission Zhang wanted to deny, but her lips parted for him and her tongue met his eagerly. His kiss softened and the invasion turned more playful. Their tongues danced and teased.

He broke off the kiss and rested his forehead on hers. "Just say yes, Zhang," he said raggedly.

Her own breathing was labored, but she glared up at him. "Never."

"Your resistance will only make our wedding night that

much sweeter," he growled into her ear. "Is that what you're hoping for? Are we continuing your fantasy?"

She pushed against his chest. "You can't be serious. I stopped playing the moment you locked me in." Her hand stilled as she sought to make him see reason. "Don't do this. I can deal with the bad press. I'll even do what I can to help you smooth it over here. This isn't you, Rachid. You know you have to let me go."

He set her back but held on to her waist. The lines of his face deepened. "You're wrong. This is exactly who I am, Zhang." His expression softened and he said, "You could be happy here, if you let yourself be."

She raised her chin defiantly and threatened, "I don't want to hurt anyone, but it'll happen if you continue on this path."

He pulled out the chair for her to sit in again and murmured, "You are so beautiful."

Shock held Zhang immobile. *Did he just go there? Did he just say I'm beautiful when I'm angry? When did my life morph into some cheesy romance novel?* Her hands clenched at her sides. "You have clearly forgotten who you're dealing with if you think a compliment can sway me. I don't care if you find me attractive, I just want to leave."

He ran a hand lightly down one of her tense arms. "Little liar. The angrier you pretend to be the more I want to prove to you how little of it is real. If you don't want me to take you right now on the table, I'd suggest you calm down."

She shook her head. Images of the two of them frantically sweeping the dishes aside and pulling off each other's clothing warmed her cheeks, and for a moment she refused to look at Rachid. A part of her wanted to push him to the place he threatened to go. There was no use pretending otherwise to herself. Frustrated, she directed her next admonishment to her loins.

Stop acting like he's the last man on the planet.
You were perfectly fine before him.
We don't need him.

Oh, my God, I'm talking to my genitalia now.

I guess I only have to worry if it answers me.

Zhang almost chuckled at the insanity of her inner dialogue.

"Zhang?" Rachid's query prompted her to look up at him.

She met his eyes reluctantly, trying but not succeeding to glare at him.

"Sit," he said, and then he gave her one of those devastatingly sexy smiles, as if he knew exactly the inner debate that was raging within her.

Zhang didn't return his smile or move to obey his command. "I'd like to go back to my room now," she said and added, "alone."

"Of course," he said, and went to the door to call a guard over to escort her back. As she passed by him, he said softly, "Don't worry, Zhang, there'll be other tables."

She grit her teeth and followed the guard out of the room, without giving Rachid the pleasure of knowing his taunt had sent another wave of warmth to her cheeks.

When she was once again locked behind the large wooden double doors of her room, Zhang removed the lace dress and threw it on the floor, as if doing so could undo the last half hour.

I'm not staying.

No man, not even that one, is worth my freedom.

She chose a long green Indian-style cotton kurta with matching pantalets and stood in front of the full-length mirror in the room-size closet. The kurta's high collar covered her neck and its long sleeves hid her arms, but the style was still distinctly, sensually feminine.

Did I really expect a change of clothing would stop my heart from racing every time I think of Rachid? I doubt even camouflage could hide the excitement in my eyes. No wonder he never believes me when I tell I don't want him.

If I'm going to escape, I have to spend less time with the reason I want to stay.

Chapter Ten

Rachid was in his private quarters a few hours later when the head of the Royal Guardsmen knocked on his door. "Your Highness, there is a Mr. Corisi down in the foyer. He wishes to speak with you."

Dominic? Isn't he supposed to be on his honeymoon?

Rachid said firmly, "Tell him that I will be down in a few minutes." He knew that whatever had happened downstairs had been serious in nature if it necessitated Marshid to become personally involved. The man added, "He's not a patient man. It was difficult to persuade him to wait to be announced."

I can imagine.

"I'll be right there."

What would have brought Dominic to Najriad? Zhang? Was there no end to the punishment for one night's pleasure? Friendships, even ones as old as theirs, could be lost over events such as this.

Rachid found his old college friend in the foyer, flanked by two armed guards.

When Dominic made a move toward Rachid, one of the guards pointed his rifle at Dominic's chest.

Dominic asked angrily, "Do all of your friends receive this warm welcome?"

"Only the ones who don't call first," Rachid said calmly in English and held up a hand to wave the guardsmen back. At first neither guard moved and Rachid's temper flared. He ordered in Arabic, "Lower your weapons now."

They did so, but with obvious reluctance.

Dominic said, "You know why I'm here. Where's Zhang?"

Rachid said smoothly, "She's safe."

Dominic's snarl deepened. "Not good enough. I want to see her."

"This is none of your business, Dominic."

Dominic took an aggressive step closer and said, "When you take a woman from my wedding and ruin my honeymoon, it damn well is my business. Abby isn't going to calm down until she knows that Zhang is okay." He looked like a bull about to charge. "When Abby isn't happy, I'm not happy. Get Zhang down here."

"That's not possible," Rachid said. Dominic's anger was an unwelcome and possibly explosive complication. His future bride needed a few more days before she was going to do anything except demand her immediate release.

And that's not going to happen.

Dominic's temper rose and his hands fisted at his sides. "I don't think you understand that I'm not asking."

Rachid's quickly mounting impatience added an edge to his words. "I have great respect for you, Dominic. We've known each other a long time. Curb your temper, friend. You won't win here."

A red flush spread across Dominic's face. "You're playing a dangerous game, Rachid."

Rachid shook his head sadly. "I'm not playing, Dom. Come back on Saturday if you wish to support Zhang. You will be welcome at our wedding dinner."

"Wedding? What the hell are you talking about?"

"I've asked Zhang to marry me."

"And she said yes?"

Not exactly.

"She will," Rachid said confidently, even though he was starting to question the surety of the outcome himself. "Either way, you need to leave the palace now."

"I'm not leaving without Zhang."

"Then we have a problem."

"No, you have a problem." He reached forward to grab Rachid by the throat, but Rachid blocked his arm.

The guardsmen rushed forward to restrain Dominic.

Rachid shook his head again and said calmly, "I probably deserve the beating you'd like to give me, old friend. However, this isn't about me or you. It's bigger than either of us. Please, Zhang is safe. By the weekend, she may even be happy. Go back to your new wife. Leave before this gets ugly."

Dominic struggled against the hands that restrained him and would have done more, but the rifle to his chest stopped him. He threatened, "It's going to get ugly, Rachid. Very ugly—and likely very painful."

Putting Dominic out of the palace would result in the man returning with a vengeance before Rachid had time to change Zhang's mind. There was only one way to make sure Dominic didn't interfere. He turned to the guardsmen. "Take him to the north wing and keep him there until I send for him."

The two guards were joined by one more who continued to hold Dominic at rifle point as they dragged him from the room. Dominic didn't say anything. He didn't have to. The entire situation was quickly getting out of control. The sooner Rachid convinced Zhang that marrying him was her best option, the better.

Rachid was halfway to the women's quarters when his father stopped him in the hallway.

"Rachid, is it true that you have a man detained in the north wing?"

Rachid met his father's expression boldly. "Yes, Father."

"Dominic Corisi?" his father asked casually.

Rachid wasn't about to second-guess himself now. "Yes."

His father stepped forward and chuckled while patting his son on the shoulder. "I used to worry that you didn't have enough Najriad fire to rule, but I see that I was mistaken. You have more than enough."

There wasn't much about what he was doing that he was proud of, but his father's praise made Rachid stand taller. "I know what's at stake."

Nodding, Amir dropped his hand. "Yes, I can see that." He

took a step back to allow his son to pass and said, "I will be returning to my quarters unless you require them as a cell for another guest."

Rachid smiled at his father's dry humor. "The day isn't over yet. I may."

Suddenly serious, the king cautioned, "Be careful, Son. I'm here if you need me."

"I have everything under control, Father."

"Of course," his father said with a smile. "Have you won over your betrothed yet?"

Rachid smiled again. "Not yet."

His father clasped his hands behind his back and said, "Try lilies."

"Flowers?" *Really?*

"Your mother always loved them." And with that, his father turned and walked away.

Lilies.

Well, it was as good as any other idea he'd had that day.

Not one who normally spent hours on quiet reflection, Zhang found the isolation of her suite strangely calming. She couldn't contact her business team, so there wasn't much use worrying about how they were dealing with her absence. She'd hired the best and paid them well. They could keep it functioning for the short time it would take her to make her escape.

The desire to have her security team storm the walls of the castle had ebbed as the day went on. She didn't want to see anyone hurt. Not her men, not these men. Not even Rachid.

I just want to go home.

Wherever the hell that is.

The sound of a key in the lock jolted Zhang. She spun toward the opening door. A tiny older woman who looked to be in her seventies entered. She was dressed in a long Western-style lavender gown that was obviously haute couture despite its simple lines. She approached Zhang with both hands outstretched. "So, this is the woman who has set my household off balance."

Zhang didn't take the hand the woman offered, but her resistance didn't seem to offend her. She walked over to one of the chaises and settled herself gracefully down upon it. Then she patted her lap and waved toward a nearby chair. "Come and talk with me."

Reluctantly, Zhang took the seat across from her. Perhaps this woman could be persuaded to release her. Only a fool let pride forfeit an opportunity.

"My name is Hadia. You may call me that." She smiled at Zhang impishly. "Or 'Grandmother,' if you prefer."

Zhang choked a bit on that. She quickly recovered her composure and said, "Hadia—that's a beautiful name."

The older woman smiled. "Thank you. Now, tell me what foolishness is going on under this roof. The men would have me believe that my grandson kidnapped you from a wedding, but I know Rachid and he would never behave so irresponsibly."

"You don't know him as well as you think."

A wise glint lit Hadia's eyes. "You were unwilling?"

Zhang looked away and blushed. "I am now."

The older woman had a gentle way about her, but there was also a firmness behind her questions. "So, you have a man who waits for you back in China?"

Zhang shook her head.

"Or in America perhaps? Europe?"

I get it. Spare me the list of continents. "I'm single," Zhang clarified.

"Then you think you can find better than my grandson? A taller man? One more handsome?" Hadia's eyes narrowed. "You think you will find a more honorable one?"

Frustrated, Zhang snapped, "How about a less insufferably controlling one? A husband of my choosing won't be quite so quick to lock me up like I'm a piece of property he doesn't want to lose."

89

"And if you were not locked in?"

"I would leave."

"Then perhaps my grandson is wise to remove the weight of that option from you."

Zhang glared at Rachid's grandmother. "What is wrong with the women here? How can you agree with how I'm being treated?"

"Is he mistreating you? Are there bruises beneath the silk he adorns you with?"

Zhang sighed. "No. However, I don't want to be here. Isn't that enough?"

The older woman smoothed the material of her gown. "Normally, yes, but you need to look outside of yourself for a moment and see the larger situation."

Zhang stood and her voice rose with irritation. "What I see clearly is that Rachid doesn't care what I want, only what's best for him."

Hadia raised one shoulder slightly and said, "A man with his back against a wall must make difficult decisions. Rachid is fighting for more than his title. The very future of Najriad is in danger. He isn't asking you to give up more than he has. Are you so important that your inconvenience is worth the lives that will be lost if our borders fail?"

Zhang fought the pull of Hadia's words. She didn't want to picture Rachid as a hero. It was easy to walk away when she imagined Rachid as a coward, but to know that he was willing to sacrifice his freedom for his people was heartbreaking and only made her resolve more painful to maintain. It also reminded her that he wanted to marry her for political reasons and not because he couldn't imagine his life without her. "A marriage wouldn't be a mere inconvenience for me. I have a company to run and people who rely on me. If we discussed this rationally, we might come up with a way to smooth the situation over without this extreme solution."

"There is nothing rational about war, Zhang, and that is what our country is on the verge of."

"And marrying me does what—gives Rachid access to money to fund his defense?"

"Money isn't what my grandson needs from you," Hadia said vaguely.

Zhang sat beside Hadia again. *I want to believe that.* "Really? He's already talking about taking control of my company. He said he would remove that worry from me."

Hadia shook her head in sympathy. "Perhaps it's because of my age, but I no longer put much merit in what a person says. If you want to know what is in a man's heart, look to his actions. My grandson built his fortune with hard work and integrity. He has remained loyal to family and country. Now he intends to marry you. I don't believe that he would take advantage of your situation to rob you."

"Even with his back against the wall? I'm sorry, I don't share your faith in humanity." Zhang felt for the woman across from her, so she shared more than she normally would have. "I fought too hard for my independence—no one is going to take that away from me."

Hadia leaned forward and put a key in Zhang's hand. She stood slowly. "I dismissed the guard from your door. There is a phone in the room across the hall and a car at the bottom of the left stairway. The driver is loyal to me and will take you wherever you ask. If you leave."

Zhang's hand closed over the key. "Thank you." She stood and squared her shoulders. "I'm sorry that I couldn't help you. It's not my war to fight."

"Of course," the woman said sadly. "If you're here tomorrow, I'll give you a tour of Nilon and you'll see what Rachid is willing to fight so hard to save."

The key dug into Zhang's clenched hand. "I won't be here."

The woman touched Zhang's shaking hand softly. "Promise me that you will do one thing before you leave."

I can't promise to see Rachid again. I would never hide my intention from him.

91

"If I can," Zhang answered honestly.

Hadia gave her hands a last supportive squeeze and said, "Call your parents, then make your decision."

That was the last thing she would have thought the grandmother would ask of her. *Call first. Call after. What did it matter? It was an easy promise to make, and one that remarkably satisfied the woman enough to leave her.*

Zhang stood in the middle of the room with the key biting into the soft flesh of one hand, long after Hadia had gone. *I'm free.* She walked through the open door and crossed the hallway to where she found a phone, just as Hadia had promised.

Mom, Dad, a funny thing happened at the wedding I went to this weekend.

No, that's not right.

Mom, I'm okay. Stop crying. I'm fine.

Sorry about the whole global-shame thing I brought upon our family.

Zhang sighed and reached for the phone.

There really is no chance that they are going to take this news well, is there?

Her mother answered in a Beijing dialect. "Zhang! We expected to hear from you yesterday."

Zhang looked at the ceiling and chose only bits of the truth. "I was busy."

"You're always busy, but this is news that a family shouldn't hear from a stranger."

"Mother," Zhang chose her words carefully, "not everything is as it was presented to you."

Xiaoli's voice went up several hysterical octaves. "You're not going to marry the prince?"

Here it comes.

"He's not the man for me, Mother. I am leaving today and —"

Her mother cut her off. "Not the man for you? There is no

man who is good enough for you, is there? Xin wasn't good enough. More than a billion people in China and you couldn't find one here. You had to choose a foreign man I won't be able to speak to."

Zhang rubbed her forehead in irritation. "Because you refuse to learn English."

"Why should I? I never asked for any of this. I was happy in our village. This is your dream. It doesn't matter to you how it affects the rest of us. How could you do this to me? Do you care that you have humiliated me with this? I can't leave the house. You are all everyone is talking about and very few believe that you were kidnapped. They say my daughter is a whore. And now you tell me that you are not going to marry this man? Even he is not good enough for you?" The sound of her mother breaking down into tears tore at Zhang.

"Mother," Zhang said urgently, wishing she were there beside her, but knowing that even if she had been was nothing she could say that would have eased her mother's pain. Some disappointments run too deep.

"I don't know you, Zhang. I don't understand how you could do this to us," Xiaoli said tearfully, and the phone clattered as if it had dropped to the floor.

A moment later, Zhang's father was on the phone, comforting his daughter in English. "Your mother will be fine. It's a relief to hear your voice."

Zhang choked on the emotion that swelled within her.

"Is it true that you're not marrying the prince?" Qiang asked.

Was there a right answer to that question?

"Is he a cruel man?" her father asked when she didn't respond.

Thinking back over the last couple of days, Zhang knew he wasn't. He was infuriatingly sure of himself, but outside of detaining her, she couldn't fault how he had treated her. "No, Father."

"Is he an honorable man?" Qiang asked quietly.

Once again, difficult as it was to admit, Rachid's loyalty to his family and his people was something she reluctantly respected. "Yes," she whispered.

Her father's voice deepened with emotion. "You are my child, Zhang. I would do anything for you. Tell me that you have been mistreated and I will gather resources here and come for you. There will not be a corner of the planet where this Prince Rachid can hide from my vengeance. I will gladly give my last breath to save you and protect you when you return. I don't care what people say. If someone hurt you, we will stand together." Slow, hot tears poured down Zhang's face as Qiang continued to speak. "But if you went with this man willingly— if you did what people say—you need to make this right."

In a whisper, Zhang asked, "What are you saying, Father?"

She had never heard her father's voice shake, but it did when he said, "Tell me that you know this man, Zhang. Tell me this is nothing more than a staged bride-napping elopement and that you will marry him. Make this right for your mother, for our community, for me... and for yourself."

Sinking into the chair beside the phone, Zhang wiped her face dry. It didn't matter how much money she made, or how many places she went in her life, she was her father's daughter. His respect meant more to her than public opinion. His honor was worth any sacrifice. "I will," she swore as she came to a decision. "Tell Mother that she'll need to go shopping because she is going to attend a royal wedding."

A moment of silence followed. Then her father said, "You will make a fine princess, Daughter."

Zhang laughed, even though she found little humor in his words. "I'm sure I'll be one they'll remember."

"Don't be sad, Zhang. You need a good man."

I thought I did.

This wasn't quite how I imagined it, though.

You have to be very careful when you make wishes—and apparently be quite specific.

Dear Universe, I'd like to submit a short amendment to my

earlier request. Is it at all possible to find love and not be asked to give up everything I've worked so hard for?

No answer came, but she hadn't expected it to.

I have to stop wasting time asking for the impossible and imagining there is a greater design to all this chaos. I'm on my own, just as I've always been.

This will only be as bad as I let it get.

Rachid's first offer had been for a temporary marriage, one that would appease public opinion and allow us to divorce in a year. I should have accepted that offer, but perhaps it's not too late. He needs me to agree to marry him and doesn't know that I've decided to marry him. I built a billion-dollar company from nothing, surely I can negotiate my way out of this.

Six months.

A contract that protects my assets.

"I'll call you soon with more details about this week," Zhang told her father and hung the phone up. Slowly, she crossed the hall again, re-entered her suite and locked the door behind her.

I'm getting married on Saturday.

Married.

Images of Rachid flashed through her mind. His surprised expression when she'd impulsively kissed him at the wedding. His relaxed, proud features as he slept beside her on the plane. That quick, sexy smile. The deep rumble of his laughter when she teased him. His amusement when she threatened him.

She turned the key over in her hand thoughtfully. A memory of crying out Rachid's name as he thrust into her again and again, bringing her to a dizzying height of passion, sent a tingle of heat through her. Could a temporary marriage be a passionate one? She steeled herself against a wave of longing.

No, that would be a dangerous mistake.

A woman could lose herself in a bargain like that. Better to keep the arrangement as business-like as possible.

Zhang hid the key in one of the drawers of a bureau near the door.

If I'm not smart about this, I could lose everything.

Chapter Eleven

Zhang was perched on one of the chairs in the parlor of her suite when she heard the door open. She didn't look up from the floor. She'd spent the last few hours mentally rehearsing exactly what she would say to Rachid.

Would he be angry or relieved?

"Zhang?" Rachid asked softly, but she still didn't turn. It wasn't like her to delay the unpleasant, but she knew that things would change between them as soon as she said her peace. He'd no longer have a reason to pretend she was anything more to him than a mistake that he was going to marry for political reasons. No matter what he said or how much it hurt, it was better than continuing this illusion that there was anything between them.

Still, there was something about his concern, even if it might be forced, that she craved. What would it be like to be loved, truly loved, by a man who was her equal? In the safety of that love, would she find a place where she didn't have to be strong every moment of the day?

He squatted down in front of her and cupped her face gently in one hand. When she refused to meet his eyes, he laid a small bouquet on her lap and said, "I brought these for you."

Tangible evidence of how far he was willing to take this farce. Next he would proclaim that he loved her and really break her heart. She took a shaky breath and gathered her resolve.

He took both of her hands in his and said softly, "Don't be sad, Zhang. Throw the flowers in my face. I like it better when you hate me."

She shook her head sadly and touched the delicate white petals absently. "I don't hate you. I want to hate you, but I don't. I did this to myself."

Without warning or permission, he scooped her up and settled her across his lap on the chair. Every muscle in Zhang tensed at the conflicting emotions that shot through her. Part of her wanted to fight, scream at him to put her down. Part of her wanted to throw her arms around him and never let him go.

He wrapped his arms around her waist and tucked her head beneath his chin. "I'm as at fault as you are," he said huskily.

Zhang sighed and allowed herself a moment of comfort. What if this was all she'd ever have? She should savor the last moments of it. She fought a sudden desire to rub herself wantonly against the growing proof that he was equally affected by their nearness. "I'm still angry with you."

She felt him smile into her hair. "I know."

She pulled back and looked up into his eyes. "I don't like to be told what to do."

The corners of his eyes crinkled with humor. "I would never have guessed."

Zhang shifted uncomfortably beneath the intensity of those dark and dangerous eyes. *Just say it. Just tell him and then explain the new rules to him.*

He groaned and said, "Don't move. I can't concentrate when you do that, and we have to talk."

Talking is overrated.

The evidence of his need for her was pulsing beneath her, sending her own heart beating at a dizzying rate. She looked down to hide her own mounting excitement. Her body clenched and moistened in memory of how expertly he had explored and teased every corner of her body. She knew the power of his back muscles as they rippled beneath her hands, the taste of his skin, the heat of his breath tickling her intimately. Too clearly, she remembered the shudder he gave just before his release.

I need to tell him that I'll marry him—as long as there are certain conditions to the agreement. First rule: none of this. This is just torture.

"Are you listening to anything I'm saying, Zhang?" he

murmured into her ear.

"Yes," she lied boldly.

He chuckled softly and kissed her neck. Zhang couldn't suppress the shiver that rocked through her. "Would it be so bad to spend each night in my arms? Marry me and we can continue what we started on our first night together."

"If I marry you," Zhang started to say, her voice husky with the passion she was about to deny.

His sexy smile shook her resolve. He ran a hand through her hair, looking far too pleased with himself. "*If*—I see we're making progress."

She took his hand in hers to cease the distraction. "I'm willing to negotiate the terms of how it could be possible." His free hand settled on one of her thighs and began a gentle caress that scrambled Zhang's thoughts for a moment. She trapped that offender beneath her other hand and said, "You originally said we could marry and divorce within a year. Six months would be better for me." She placed both of his hands on the arms of the chair they sat in and held them there. "And it would be best if we kept things platonic between us. Sex is only going to confuse the situation."

He grew very still. "Are those all of your conditions?" There was something dangerous in his softly spoken question.

She met his eyes boldly. "No. I also want you to sign a contract that protects my company, Eight Lions Developments, from your interference or ownership. I don't need your help running it. I can rely heavily on my team for a while if I have to, but I can't hand over control of my company to anyone."

He tensed beneath her like a cat preparing to pounce. "Is that it?"

His expression was impossible to read. "Yes," Zhang said.

Would he agree?

Would he come back with terms of his own?

She waited and forgot to breathe.

"I will sign a contract that protects your assets. You don't trust me yet and there likely isn't time to rectify that before we marry."

Zhang let out a sigh of relief.

He freed one hand and rubbed one thumb possessively over her jawline. "There is a problem, however, with the rest of your conditions."

Zhang gulped and waited.

"You're mine now, Zhang, and our marriage will be a real one." He leaned down and whispered against her lips. "I will have you in my bed every night." With a gentle turn of her head he gave himself access to her neck, and his hot breath tickled it as he laid verbal claim to her. "I will find pleasure in your body as you will find pleasure in mine. Mine will be the only name you will ever call out in ecstasy. You belong to me now."

That sounds heavenly.

Zhang shook her head.

No, that sounds dangerous. I've worked way too hard for my independence to trade it for a lifetime of orgasms.

Amazing, earthshaking, toe-curling orgasms.

"I don't belong to anyone," Zhang denied, but her voice was thick with passion. "Six months is all I can give you, and sex is not part of the deal."

His other hand snuck up one leg and slipped beneath the material of her dress, laying claim to one of her thighs for a moment, then moving higher. Warm, firm and seeking. He whispered, "Then we'll have to renegotiate the terms, won't we?"

His mouth was on hers, demanding a response that Zhang found she could not deny. His tongue swept into her mouth, teasing, claiming. Zhang met his thrusting tongue with her own, fighting not to lose herself. She shuddered as his thumb eased the silk of her panties aside and began to rhythmically caress her nub.

Giving in to him now would be a real mistake.

Some mistakes were too good not to make.

She eased her legs apart slightly to allow him better access. The rhythm of his caress increased and a slow warmth began to build within her. "Why try to deny what's between us?" Rachid murmured. "You want this as much as I do."

Coherent arguments dissolved as his index finger joined his thumb and began to gently stroke her most sensitive spot. Heat ripped through her at a level almost too intense to be pleasurable. She gripped his forearm with one hand as her resolve melted.

A lifetime of this might not be as bad as I imagine.

"Marry me. Keep your company, but give me this," he whispered against her mouth. Zhang shuddered with pleasure when he slid one finger inside of her and rolled it gently, continuing a steady external rhythm with his thumb. "Give yourself to me."

He pulled one side of her dress aside and began to tease her breast through the lace of her bra, alternating warm, wet circles with gentle suckling. His hot breath was ragged against her, matching her own frantic breathing as she let go and began to writhe against his talented fingers.

He slid a second finger within her and began to pump them slowly in and out. Unable to think clearly, Zhang grabbed his face between both of her hands and met his mouth urgently with her own. He was deep in her mouth and deep in her folds when a white heat began to build and spread through her abdomen. Her breath caught in her throat and she clenched on his fingers.

He broke the kiss and whispered, "Say yes, Zhang."

She threw her head back in abandon as hot wave after wave of pleasure rocked her body. She cried out twice, "Yes, yes..." and again, louder, as she climaxed: "Yes!" As secondary shudders of pleasure shook her, his hand closed possessively on her moist center.

As far as proposals went, his technique was improving.

He nuzzled her neck and said, "You're mine, Zhang." His excitement was still hard and pulsing beneath her. He took her hand and adjusted their position so that he could press her hand to him. "Feel what you do to me." He rubbed her hand against his shaft. "Your fantasy has become mine."

101

She pulled her hand away, but it was shaking from the mix of emotions rushing through her. *Boundaries. We need boundaries.* "I also fantasize about being in charge."

His eyes burned with a deepening desire. "I might enjoy that, too." His sexy chuckle confused her.

She tried to stand, but he held her in his lap. "This isn't funny."

He slid a hand inside her open bodice, beneath the lace of her bra, and cupped her small breast. "I wasn't joking." Looking deep into her eyes, he gently teased her nipple between his fingers, smiling as it hardened beneath his attention.

Despite the growing sensations that threatened to drown her again, Zhang raised her chin proudly and said, "Six months, Rachid."

"I can work with that," he murmured, a patient smile teasing his lips.

She stiffened and pushed his hand away. "I'm serious. And we can't do this anymore."

He laughed, stood and took her hand. "Come, I have a guest downstairs who needs to see you before he will leave without a fight."

Zhang nodded without even bothering to ask who the guest was.

How am I going to be able to convince him that I don't want this if I keep turning to putty in his hands every time he reaches for me?

He guided her down the hallway with a light touch to her lower back. She looked over her shoulder and met his eyes. His smile revealed that he knew exactly what he was doing to her. He said, "I'm not supposed to be in the women's quarters, and you can't sleep in my suite until we're married. This week can't pass fast enough for me."

Me either.

See, that's not helping.

I have to be stronger than that.

We need to stop this before one of us forgets how

impossible this situation is and that we are wrong for each other.

They didn't make it to the end of the hallway before Rachid stopped and backed her against the wall. "One last kiss to tide me over."

His lips swept down and claimed hers again. She wrapped her arms around his neck.

I'm definitely going to set him straight.

Later.

Chapter Twelve

"I told Abby you didn't want to be rescued!" Dominic cursed for a long, colorful moment. One side of his face was red, and there was a beginning of a bruise developing around one of his eyes.

Rachid stood beside Zhang, his hand still resting lightly on her lower back. Tension held her muscles tight, the only indication that his future wife was uncomfortable in the face of Dominic's anger. Rachid said, "Calm yourself, Dominic."

"Was a phone call too much to ask for? I don't care what you do with your life, Zhang, but you had everyone upset."

Zhang said, "Dominic, I'm —"

Feeling fiercely protective suddenly, Rachid said, "The fault is mine, Dom." He took a deep breath and reminded himself of his friend's good intentions. "I do appreciate your loyalty to Zhang."

Something in his tone reached Dominic. He said, "You can thank me by telling these goons to put their weapons down."

Rachid nodded at the guardsmen and they reluctantly pointed their rifles to the floor. He studied his friend's face and said, "You're lucky you didn't get killed. These men have orders to protect the royal family at all costs."

Dominic rubbed his swelling face and glared at one of the guards. "Some enjoy that job more than others."

Rachid made note of what Dominic said. He would talk to the head of security later. "Leave us," he said to the guards.

They hesitated.

Rachid repeated the order. "I said—leave us."

"Yes, Your Highness," one said, and the others echoed his words.

As the guard on his left passed, Dominic's fist flew up in a backward blow that connected with the man's face and sent him stumbling to the side. The two other guards jumped in reaction but were halted by a command Rachid issued in Arabic. "This man is a guest and one who has not been treated well in his short stay. Do not confuse the volume of my voice with leniency. I have more of my father in me than you know. You would be wise to remember that."

His warning gained the respect his mere presence should have. The guards bowed in apology and made a hasty retreat.

Zhang shook her head and said, "I have to learn Arabic."

Dominic brushed a speck of something off his jacket arm as if he were brushing off the offensive presence of those who had left. He said, "Some things don't require translation. At least now I know he wasn't acting on your orders." There was still an angry light in his eyes. "That doesn't make us even though, Rachid. You went too far this time."

Rachid met his friend's anger with confidence and spoke from his heart. "I went exactly as far as I needed to go, Dom. I'm fighting for my family here. You can help or you can leave, but be warned that I am capable of going much further if the situation requires it. When it comes to protecting those I care about, my morality is—flexible. This is something you should understand well."

Dominic appeared to weigh this new side of a friend he thought he knew. "Is it safe to bring Abby here? Because there is no way she is not going to want to attend your wedding."

"My security will be at your disposal," Rachid assured him.

Dominic touched the growing bruise on one of his temples and let the action express his faith in how that would work out for him.

Rachid said, "There will be no repeat of today. I'll make sure of that. If told to, my men would die to protect you."

Dominic nodded but added, "I'd still like to bring a few of my own people. Just in case."

"Of course," Rachid said. "I will have a section of the palace prepared for you. You may set it up with whatever security you wish." A thought occurred to him and he asked, "You came alone today?"

Dominic merely smiled. "Yes, this was personal."

Rachid laughed. "You are one crazy bastard."

Dominic smiled. "Hey, I'm not the one marrying Zhang. Do you know she sent a squadron of men with machine guns to my island?"

She what? He'd heard bits and pieces of that story at the wedding but hadn't made the connection to the small woman at his side. It was difficult to reconcile the image of her gloriously naked and playfully laughing with him on his plane, with the knowledge that she was one of the few people on the planet who had ever taken Dominic on directly. It's likely she would have won had Abby not called her off.

Zhang smiled up at his frown as if she knew his thoughts and was enjoying his moment of discomfort. He unleashed his change of temper on his friend. "You will speak of her with respect, Dominic, or you will not be welcome in my home."

Dominic's eyebrows rose in surprise. "She's not that easy to offend."

Rachid's hand dropped from Zhang's back and he stepped toward Dominic aggressively. "I am."

Zhang asked, sounding somewhat amused, "Is this really necessary?"

Absolutely.

Rachid said, "This doesn't concern you, Zhang."

"I'd say it does," she said sarcastically.

Rachid deliberately invaded Dominic's personal space and said, "Dom and I are clarifying a few things."

Dominic held his friend's angry look, then his face relaxed into a smile and he put a hand on Rachid's shoulder. "Okay," he said and nodded.

And just like that, the storm passed.

Rachid mirrored his gesture, then stepped back and said,

"Come, Dominic. My father will want to meet you."

He returned to Zhang's side and guided her down one of the hallways. He felt her glance at him repeatedly and knew she wanted to say something to him. He bent to her level as they walked so she could share without being overheard.

She said, "I don't need you to protect me."

His hand caressed her lower back as she spoke. "As my wife, you will always be under my protection. Your honor is my honor. Dominic understands that now."

She stiffened beneath his touch. "And if I want to fight my own battles?"

Rachid smiled. "Then we will spend many nights making up until you understand our ways." The thought sent a wave of excitement through him. "Which may not be a bad thing."

Zhang glared at him, but he saw the answering passion behind her mask of strength.

He handed her off to one of the guards, who he instructed in Arabic to bring her back to her quarters. "It's not necessary to lock her in," he added and found his own directions reassuring.

In English, he said, "Zhang, there is a phone across the hall from your room. You may make all the calls you require."

He wasn't sure what to think of the smile she flashed him as she said, "How kind of you."

He watched her walk away, mesmerized by the gentle sway of her hips, and told himself he wasn't disappointed that she didn't turn around one last time before she disappeared around the corner.

Dominic rocked back on his heels thoughtfully and said, "You're playing with fire with that one, Rachid."

Rachid glared at his amused friend. "I know what I'm doing."

Dominic shook his head and put a supportive hand on his friend's shoulder. "I'm becoming quite reflective as I get older, and I just realized that love and loss share some of the same stages. You are definitely in denial."

"I'm not in love," Rachid said curtly.

Dominic laughed. "Famous last words. Come on, let's go see your father. I have a honeymoon to return to."

As they walked, Rachid said, "You're wrong this time, Dominic."

Like the rest of the palace, the king's suite was a combination of old-world workmanship and modern luxury. He was a wealthy man who used part of his private quarters to entertain political leaders from around the world, so his sitting room was a cream-and-gold showpiece. He smiled when he saw his son and waved for Rachid and his friends to enter. "I see you have brought me more company," Amir said, gesturing toward the other men in the room. "I would have ordered entertainment had I known the celebrations were starting this soon."

Rachid said, "Father, I should have told you..."

His father dismissed his son's concerns with a wave of his hand. "Don't worry, Son, I am finding each guest more interesting than the last." He sat and encouraged the group to take seats. Only one did. Amir gestured to the older man who had taken the seat to his right. "Mr. Andrade and his son, Stephan, are here to discuss a possible business opportunity. Mr. Walton says that he received a disturbing text from a friend he thought was in danger, but who I see now is..." He paused as he took in the bruises on Dominic's face, then added, "No longer a point of concern."

Dominic scowled at Jake. "It took you long enough to get here." When he saw the half-eaten plate of fruit in front of his business partner, he asked sarcastically, "How was lunch?"

Jake didn't look bothered by his friend's irritation. "I was in London when I found out you'd come here. You're lucky that I was already on my way when I received your text."

"Lucky?" Dominic asked. "My version of a rescue mission doesn't include a snack."

Jake smiled. "Diplomacy, Dominic. I wasn't leaving without you."

Dominic turned to the blond man in the room and boomed out another question: "Did you come to save me, too, Stephan?"

Stephan took a moment to study the marks on Dominic's face and his mouth twitched with humor he tried to contain. "I was invited. I'm not sure what happened to you, but my visit has been quite pleasant so far."

Dominic reached forward and grabbed the man by his shirt collar. Instead of cowering as some might have, Stephan burst out laughing. "Dominic, I can't... I can't pretend the idea of you being held by Najriad's royal security isn't funny."

When Dominic's left hand pulled back to punch the humor out of his old adversary, Stephan only laughed more and raised one hand in a mockery of defending himself. "Remember your sister, Dom. She doesn't like it when we fight."

With a grunt of frustration, Dominic shoved a still-smiling Stephan away from him. "You'll push me too far one day, Stephan."

Stephan straightened his clothing, not looking the least bit concerned. "Is it my fault that you're so easy to bait?"

Jake moved between the two men. "This isn't helping anyone."

Stephan said, "Five minutes ago you found humor in the situation. Don't pretend you didn't."

Rachid stepped into the mix. "Perhaps we should move on to a less exciting topic."

Jake said, "Like what we're all doing here? I left Lil in London, but she's worried about Zhang."

Rachid said, "There's no reason for anyone to be concerned. Zhang and I will marry this weekend."

Jake said, "I'd like to see her if it's possible."

Dominic said, "I met with her. She's not doing it under duress."

Rachid's father said, "Of course you are all welcome to attend the wedding to see for yourselves."

Stephan said, "Are you sure Najriad can handle two visits from Dominic?"

109

Dominic made an ugly sound in his throat. "Rachid, let Stephan meet your security. Please."

Rachid laughed.

Antonio Andrade entered the testosterone-filled conversation from his seat, gently admonishing his son. "Stephan, enough. King Amir will think I raised you with no manners."

The king laughed in sympathy with his fellow father. "I have two sons. If no blood is spilled, I'm not usually concerned."

Antonio joined his laughter. "Isn't it difficult to turn the reins over when they still sound like schoolboys at times?"

Amir met his son's eyes across the room and said, "I admit to moments of concern in the past, but my son impresses me more with each passing day."

Feeling much younger than his thirty years, Rachid straightened with pride. For the first time since his father had summoned him home, he began to think he might save Najriad after all.

A short time later, Stephan and his father stood and shook hands with the king and Rachid. Stephan said, "Thank you. We have all of the information we need, and we'll send you over some proposals based on what we discussed earlier."

Antonio said, "We don't expect a quick response since this is sure to be a busy week for your family. Please contact either of us if you have any questions."

As Stephan passed Dominic, he said, "Do you need a ride home?"

Dominic shook his head and said, "Say hello to Nicole for me."

Antonio shook Dominic's hand warmly and said, "Will you return to the States before the weekend?"

Dominic said, "I'll be joining Abby in London for a few days."

Rachid called two guards over to walk Stephan and his father out.

Lil Dartley answered her phone on the fourth ring, sounding as flustered as she normally did, which was oddly reassuring. Parts of Zhang's world might be entirely upside down, but Lil was proof that some of it was still intact.

"Lil," Zhang started but was quickly overridden by her friend.

"Oh, my God, Zhang! Are you all right?" Lil raised her voice and said loudly, "Abby, it's Zhang!"

Zhang groaned. "I was hoping to speak with you privately."

Lil made a dramatic correction to her sister. "No, no, I didn't say Zhang. I said... Stan?"

Zhang heard Abby say, "You are the world's worst liar, Lil. If that's Zhang, can you ask her if she's okay? Then I'll leave you alone to talk to her."

Lil said nothing for a moment and then said, "This feels like one of those trick questions. If I ask her how she's doing you're going to know it's Zhang."

Abby said, "I already do."

Lil's voice deepened with irritation. "She wants to talk to me privately."

"What if she needs help and only has one minute to tell us before they catch her?"

In a rush, Lil said, "Oh, shit, I didn't think of that. Zhang, are you okay? Say something."

Zhang smiled into the phone. "I miss you two." She rolled her eyes in resignation. "Put me on speakerphone."

Abby said, "Dom and I were in South America when we saw the photos. What happened, Zhang? The news said that you were taken against your will. We tried to contact you and when you didn't answer your phone I knew something was wrong. Dominic sent me to London to meet up with Lil and went on to Najriad."

Lil said, "Jake should be there by now, too."

Zhang said, "I only saw Dominic."

Abby said, "And he's fine? He was so angry I was afraid he was going to do something dangerous and get himself killed."

Zhang remembered the bruises on his face but kept that to herself. Abby would only worry more. "He and Rachid were going to see his father when I left them."

Lil said, "Knowing Jake, he is probably having lunch with the king." Zhang had to admit that Lil's guess was probably right on target. If Jake was in Najriad, he would be smoothing things over.

Too late to save her, but sweet nonetheless.

Abby said, "I hated to see him go, but I'll never forget how you came for me when I needed you." She paused, then asked, "If you're not in any danger, why didn't you answer your phone?"

Lil reluctantly added, "I have her phone."

Abby's voice rose as she asked, "You have her phone and you didn't tell me? Wait, why do you have Zhang's phone?" She directed her next question to Zhang. "Why does she have your phone?"

Zhang opened her mouth to answer, but as usual, the Americans supplied their own answers. Abby said, "Lil, what did you do?"

Lil said, "I may have dared her to kiss Rachid."

Abby sighed. "Lil, how could you?"

Lil defended herself. "I just said 'kiss.' I don't know what they were doing in that photo, but none of that was my fault."

Zhang cut in. "Abby, don't blame your sister. I took the dare. I left with Rachid. Neither of us noticed the photographer. Lil's idea just got a little out of hand."

"That's nothing new," Abby said. "Lil, you ruined my honeymoon."

Lil didn't sound contrite when she answered, "You can afford another one. How many chances was Zhang going to have to kiss a hot sheikh?"

During the ensuing pause in the sisters' conversation, Zhang said, "I am sorry about your honeymoon, Abby. I know this will delay it even further, but I'm calling to invite both of you to a wedding dinner on Saturday."

For one blissful moment, both women were quiet. Then Lil burst out, "Are you getting married, Zhang?"

Zhang almost laughed at the excitement in the young woman's voice.

Abby sounded much more cautious. "Is this what you want, Zhang? If it's not, we can fix this. I don't know how, but I'm sure there is something we can do."

Lil said, "I have to hear how he proposed! It must have been amazing for you to say yes."

Abby said, "Lil, she didn't know him before our wedding. Do you honestly think they are in love?"

Lil defended her enthusiasm. "You decided to marry Dominic after a week."

Abby said, "That was different."

Lil said, "Sure, so different. Let's see. You hooked up with Dominic, flew to another country with him, the world thought he'd kidnapped you, but you were really in love with him and ready to marry him. I can see how this is totally different."

Abby sighed and then laughed. "I hate when you're so wrong and so right at the same time. It makes arguing with you very hard."

Lil laughed too. "Just because I see things differently doesn't make my view wrong. Now, can we get back to Zhang? Zhang, are you still there?"

Zhang chuckled. "Yes, I'm here."

Lil asked, "You're not being forced to marry Rachid, are you, Zhang?"

Zhang hesitated. She doubted either of these women would understand how honor trumped personal happiness. Americans saw themselves as individuals, responsible only for their own happiness. They prided themselves on their independence. Even though there were parts of her culture that she had defied, family honor was still as important to Zhang as her own life was. She knew Rachid felt the same. Beyond that, it wasn't as if she could explain the tangled sexual web she'd woven for herself. So she simply said, "No one is forcing me."

Abby asked, "You're happy?"

Yes would have been a lie. "I want to marry him."

Abby said, "It seems so sudden." From the worried tone in her voice, it was clear that she was still unconvinced.

Lil said, "Well, I think it's romantic. And we get to attend a second wedding in one week!" She thought about it and asked, "Zhang, can we do that henna thing? You know, how they do those temporary tattoos?"

Zhang said, "The wedding is going to be very small. Family and a few friends. It's more of a formality than a celebration. I doubt we'll follow many traditions on either side."

Lil pressed, "You only get married once. Why not enjoy it?"

Lil had a point. Yes, there were aspects of the wedding that she had no control over, but why not enjoy what she could? It was time to give the palace staff something to do besides guard her.

Zhang said, "If you come on Friday, I'll have a henna party with you both."

"Really?"

"Sure."

Abby said, "That's not necessary, Zhang. It's your wedding. You don't have to do anything special for us to attend."

Zhang said, "I don't have to—I want to."

Lil said, "Abby, relax. This will be fun. And I bet Zhang is looking for a way to keep her mind off everything that's going on." Zhang didn't deny the claim, and Lil continued. "Abby doesn't think like us, Zhang. Dominic is the only wild choice she's ever made."

"Us?" Zhang asked.

Lil said, "I knew when I first met you that we were kindred

souls, Zhang. I know exactly how this situation made you feel when it got out of control. I do shit like this all the time. Just know that the mortification and embarrassment you feel passes. Sometimes it even turns out well. You can't let the ugly stuff they're saying about you in the news get to you."

Abby hastily put the brakes on her sister's monologue. "Lil, you're not making Zhang feel better."

Lil countered, "You don't think she's read the papers?"

Oh, Lil. Zhang said, "I appreciate what you're trying to do. No matter what the papers say, though, we're going with the story of a staged bride-napping elopement."

Lil asked, "And you want us to keep to that story?"

Harsh as it sounded, some things needed to be said. "No, I'm asking you to say nothing. Don't talk to anyone about this."

"Don't worry, Zhang."

"Lil, this is important. No one."

Lil sighed dramatically. "I made one mistake with the paparazzi and it never aired."

Zhang stressed, "Lives will be lost if you make that mistake here, Lil. This isn't Boston or New York. A mistake won't be embarrassing here, it'll be deadly."

For once, Lil didn't have a witty response.

Abby asked quietly, "Is it safe for us to come?"

Zhang said, "I wouldn't ask you if I didn't think so, but perhaps Colby shouldn't..."

Lil said, "I'll ask Marie to watch her. She loves Colby and she won't mind flying out here to do it. Jake would probably have insisted on that, anyway. I used to think he was so in control of his emotions, but you should see him melt when she cries. She knows exactly how to wrap him around her little finger. It's hilarious to watch."

Always a planner, Abby asked, "So the earliest you'd like us to come is Friday morning? We'll set up things on this end and then we can fly over early if you'd like."

As lovely as the two women were, the less time they actually spent in Najriad, the less of a chance there was that something else could go wrong. "Yes, I have things I need to do before you arrive."

Like find my sanity.

Zhang continued, "On Saturday, Rachid and I will sign various contracts with our parents. We'll actually be married then, but only our families will attend that. We will have a dinner that night to celebrate." Fresh from attending an elaborate and joyous wedding, Zhang felt that she needed to prepare her friends for the difference. Circumstances had diminished what would have been a weeklong extravaganza in Zhang's or Rachid's culture into a formal, low-key, one-day affair. Neither family was particularly proud of the publicity that surrounded their wedding day. Since the outcome would be the same, there was really no use focusing on what would have been. *If you spend your life mourning what isn't, you miss out on what is.* "It won't be like yours, Abby, but I'm pleased that you'll both attend."

"Anything special we should know?" Abby asked.

Zhang thought about it and said, "Dress conservatively. Even for the wedding. Wear something that covers your shoulders, and keep your skirts long."

Lil said, "How oppressive. I can't imagine living somewhere where I can't dress the way I want to."

Zhang said, "Different isn't better or worse, Lil. Often *better* is merely whatever you've grown up with and are used to."

Never one to hold back, Lil asked, "Are the women there treated like second-class citizens?"

Zhang answered honestly, "I haven't been here long enough to tell you how the majority of women are treated. However, I would suspect that Najriad is just like every other society—it has its strengths and it has a dark underbelly. Show me a country that doesn't have something it's ashamed of and I'll show you a people who are living a lie. There is always something beautiful and always something ugly. That's the balance of nature."

Abby interjected, "It's difficult for even me to imagine you being told what to do, Zhang."

"I'll admit that not every aspect of this will be easy for me."

Lil said, "I wish... I wish I was as good at giving advice as you are, Zhang. You really helped me understand myself better. I want to do the same for you, but I don't know what to say."

Zhang smiled gently into the phone. "Sometimes all you can do is support someone."

Abby said, "We can do that."

Putting the seriousness behind her, Lil asked, "Hey, will you have a camel at the wedding?"

Abby groaned.

Zhang laughed. "The castle we're staying in is in the middle of a large city... about the size of London. You'd have a better chance of seeing a camel in New York."

Abby added, "Not to mention, Lil, it's an awful stereotype to have of an entire region of the world that is actually quite modernized."

Lil challenged, "Are you telling me that there are no camels at all over there?"

Zhang admitted with a guilty smile that only Lil could wring from her, "I did see one near the desert castle."

Lil leapt on that one. "Desert castle! I knew it! Oh, Zhang, you are going to have to tell me everything."

Sorry, Lil, it's a bit too spicy to share.

Abby said, "Lil, some things are private."

Confidently, Lil replied, "Not between Zhang and me. We have this connection."

Zhang's smile widened and unexpected tears filled her eyes. She didn't have any female members of her family that she was close to. No one had ever spoken to her the way Lil did, and for a moment she wondered if this was how it felt to have a sister. Even though Abby and Lil bickered, did these two women realize how absolutely blessed they were have each other?

Zhang said, "I am honored that you will both attend my wedding. Abby, I do regret you cutting your honeymoon short for this."

Abby said, "Well, it's not like we were holed up in a private cabin. We were touring potential sites to build schools. As a wedding present, Dominic started an educational foundation in my name, and we're starting a program in South America. It's exciting work, but nothing that can't easily be done in a couple of weeks. Your wedding is important. Dominic will be busy with his new Chinese server the following week. I'm just happy that his impromptu visit to Najriad didn't get him in trouble."

So am I, Zhang thought.

"So, I'll see you both on Friday?" Zhang asked in closing.

Abby said, "We wouldn't miss it for the world."

Lil said, "Wait? What do you want as a wedding present?"

"I have everything I need, or almost everything," she said. "Bring my phone."

The second call Zhang made was to the head of her security team. After a brief explanation of the situation, one based on her elopement story, Zhang said abruptly, "Plant men in and around Najriad. I'm staying in the city palace in Nilon. No one can know you're here. As of now, I don't need you to do anything except stay close and ready."

When you pay someone well enough for long enough, they don't ask why—they just follow your orders. He asked, "Do you have a specific concern, or is this a precaution?"

"A precaution for now, but keep your ears open for chatter. I have a bad feeling, but I can't pin it down."

"Do you want someone in the palace?"

Zhang thought about how loyal the servants had proven to be so far and said, "Yes, but you'll have to recruit a local and be extremely generous."

Her team hadn't disappointed her yet in the six years

they'd worked for her. *I'm not a helpless captive.* It was time she showed Rachid exactly who he was marrying. A few days of being with the real her and he might quickly change his mind about how long their marriage would or wouldn't last.

Oddly, that thought saddened her more than she liked to admit.

Her third call was the one she least wanted to make. She gathered the lead team of Eight Lions Development, her real estate company, and informed them that she would be temporarily working from out of the country... very far out.

Why?

Oh, I'm getting married.

Since she didn't trust any of them enough to share the real story, the explanation was a painfully long exchange of lies and congratulations. Followed by more lies and reassurances that her marriage would only affect her ability to meet with clients for a short time.

Zhang returned to her suite, alone and tired. She slipped off her low-heel shoes and pulled the gown over her head, folding it neatly and placing it on one of the benches in her room. In just her underclothing, she padded over to the walk-in closet and chose a peach silk nightgown. A quick hot shower eased some of her tension, but her mind was still racing when she slipped into the large bed.

Alone isn't all bad.

Didn't married women complain of snoring, fighting for blankets and odd smells that were denied in the beginning of marriage and joked about as the couple became more comfortable? Her bed had been the same way for more than ten years—absolutely quiet, all hers without dispute and lightly scented by her preferred perfume—a Jasmine oil. All of that would change on Saturday night. Legally, she and Rachid would be married as soon as they signed the contracts. Rachid might wait until after the guests left on Sunday before moving her to his room, but she doubted that he'd be that patient.

One of Zhang's strengths was that she made decisions quickly. Indecision hinders action and breeds weakness. There is strength in the mere act of choosing a course and directing all of your energy toward it.

I told him that our marriage would be for six months.

I told him that I didn't want to sleep with him again.

He dismissed both ideas.

Zhang flipped over onto her stomach and punched the pillow.

Am I angry at him for not listening to me?

Or angry at myself for being happy he didn't?

Maybe it's something in the coffee, but I don't seem able to think straight in Najriad.

Tomorrow, I go back to drinking tea.

The next morning, respectfully covered in a simple blue-green ankle-length dress and matching scarf, Zhang sat across from Hadia in a small café after their tour of Nilon City. Najriad was modern in some ways and strictly traditional in others. Women of all ages were either fully covered by abayas or dressed in a more Westernized—though still modest —style, favoring high necklines, long sleeves and long hems. Zhang had asked Hadia for guidance in this matter. She didn't want her first public appearance to be an offensive one. Hadia's tour had started with a perusal of the older woman's closet.

Although Hadia was in her seventies, one wouldn't have guessed that by how she kept up to date with international fashion designers. She joked that once upon a time she'd had a closet for the street and a closet for her husband, but now she simply dressed for herself. That didn't mean she didn't show her respect for the old ways. She still kept mostly covered in public and wore a scarf over her hair.

When Zhang had chosen her clothing based on Hadia's suggestions, Hadia had commented, "When I read about your very independent life, I wasn't sure if I could see you as the queen of Najriad, but you have impressed me.

Zhang had shrugged and replied, "I walk the line between two cultures already—what is a third?"

In the café, Hadia ordered coffee and Zhang ordered sanity, a British blend of it. Hadia referenced the guards who stood nearby and asked, "Does it bother you to not be able to go out alone?"

Zhang shook her head. "I lost that privilege years ago when I had my first real taste of success. If you have something, there will always be those who wish to take it from you. I usually travel with my own security."

Hadia looked around the busy streets. "And where are these men today?"

For a woman who spent most of her days in a palace, she was sharp about the ways of the world. "They're close," Zhang admitted. She didn't doubt for a moment that had she called out in distress, one of her men would have materialized from the surrounding crowd.

Hadia nodded in approval. "So, what did you think of Nilon?"

"It's beautiful, and the focus that Rachid has placed on higher education is apparent."

"His goal is to strengthen math and science skills at all levels so that when he moves his headquarters here, our people will not only work in the city—they will invent, create and redesign our economy through innovation."

"An admirable goal."

And one much like my own.

Both gracefully thanked the young woman who served their drinks. The girl recognized the king's mother and bowed repeatedly. She was dressed in a modest, embroidered shirt and loose pants. Uncovered, her long black hair was tied neatly at her neck. Earlier, Hadia had explained that the rules for the youth were changing—something she was both happy and concerned about. However, clothing choice was no longer the topic Hadia was interested in. She said, "My grandson takes his responsibility very seriously, but he struggles with himself. Did he tell you that his mother passed away in childbirth?"

Zhang shook her head and sipped at her black tea. The topic reminded her of how little she knew about the man she would marry in a few days.

Hadia sipped her coffee, nodded with approval to the server who retreated when she did and said, "It shaped who Rachid is, but he won't speak of it. His mother was quite controversial. She was English and no one accepted her." Hadia smiled as she remembered the woman. "My son loved her, though. For a while, I feared that he would leave us for her, but they married and she joined him here."

Zhang sat forward in her seat. "That couldn't have been easy for her."

"I imagine it wasn't. She was rigid in some of her beliefs and that made it more difficult for both of them. She loved Amir, though, and that was enough for me to accept her. The people weren't as easy to win over. She might have succeeded, but she got pregnant within their first year of marriage and was sickly through most of the pregnancy. She died before the people knew her—or she them."

"That's so sad."

Hadia put her coffee down and looked up, revealing sadness in her eyes. "It was, in more than one way. My son, Amir, took her death hard. He was angry with himself, with the people who didn't mourn her—even turned against his faith for a time. Amir couldn't bear to be with Rachid in the beginning. He said it was too painful. Sometimes I think that Rachid has spent his whole life paying the price for a tragedy that was not his fault."

"Is that why Rachid was sent away to school?" Zhang's heart broke for the little boy who'd lost everything and for the man who somehow blamed himself.

Shrugging one shoulder slightly, Hadia said, "Amir said it was because he wanted to bring technology to Najriad. His reasoning was sound, but I never agreed with the decision. Rachid was sent away at only eight years old, too young to be on his own. He should have at least brought him home each summer, but he didn't. He remarried, and perhaps it was easier for all to have Rachid out of the picture. I love my son, but Amir should have called Rachid home when Ghalil was born. Raising one son here and sending one son away has kept them strangers to each other. Strangers make easy adversaries. Ghalil has never had to compete for his father's love, and everyone believed that he would become king one day."

"Even though Rachid was the eldest?"

"In Najriad, a ruling sheikh is chosen by his family. Lineage is important, but Amir could pass his title on to a brother or a cousin as easily as he could to his children."

"Did Rachid consider turning the title down?"

"I'm sure he did. The people don't know or trust him. I've seen him struggle to express himself in Arabic. It can't be easy for him to try to prove himself worthy."

"Then why accept it? He has a successful life outside of Najriad. His brother could become king and it seems that they would both be happier." Anger surfaced for the loyalty Rachid had shown a country that thus far didn't appreciate the sacrifices he'd made for it.

Hadia took another sip of her coffee and said, "Amir chose Rachid. It's as simple as that. As far as I know, Rachid has only said no to his father one time."

Zhang raised an eyebrow in question.

"For you. Amir's original plan involved tossing you to the proverbial wolves, but Rachid wouldn't hear of it." She watched Zhang closely as she said, "He cares about you."

The news rocked Zhang's composure. Rachid had defied his father? For her? "He's only marrying me for political reasons." She clung to a theory that was becoming more and more difficult to believe.

Hadia smiled gently. "Is he? He was offered another option that would have satisfied his father and his country, but he wouldn't allow you to be publicly disgraced."

Uncomfortable with a topic that threatened to make her question the path she had set for herself, Zhang said, "Why are you telling me this?"

"Because your words say you will marry my grandson, but your eyes tell a different story."

Zhang answered stiffly while pretending to watch the people who passed by the window. "I am marrying Rachid on Saturday."

"And then?" Hadia asked.

Zhang hedged, "Does anyone know what tomorrow holds?"

"They do if they have already outlined it in their heart."

We finally come to why you wanted to see me today. Turning to look Hadia in the eye again, Zhang asked, "What do you want from me, Hadia?"

"I want my grandson to finally be happy. You think he needs this wedding to save his country, but he could easily have not married you." She leaned forward and said earnestly, "I know Rachid. When he promises you forever, he'll mean it. Will you?"

Zhang's heart pounded in her chest. She wanted to tell Hadia that none of this was her business, but it was impossible to look into those wise old eyes and do anything but tell her the truth. She whispered, "Rachid wants to control me."

Hadia suddenly looked amused. "They all try, Zhang. Would you really want a man who whimpered at your feet at the first sign of your displeasure? What fun would that man be in bed?"

Zhang flushed a deep red.

Hadia touched her hand lightly. "I've embarrassed you. That wasn't my intention. Please, forgive me."

Zhang met the older woman's eyes and said, "No apology is necessary. Your comment simply took me by surprise."

Hadia laughed. "Ah, the young always think the old were born wrinkled and chaste. Once upon a time, I married an arrogant desert prince of my own." Memories temporarily added a shine to her eyes. "I still miss him." She gripped Zhang's hand and said, "When you're my age, will your pride have given you children and grandchildren? Will the independence that you are so afraid of losing comfort you through the losses life will eventually send your way? What is all you have worth if you don't share it with someone you love?"

Zhang's throat tightened around a truth that hurt to admit even to herself. She said, "Rachid and I are not in love."

Hadia made a face. "In love. I have never liked that expression. Love isn't a bucket one can fall in and out of. Love is a seed of trust deliberately planted in commitment and friendship. If tended to with respect and passion—it flourishes. You're afraid, and that's natural—but did you let fear stop you from reaching your business goals? You can't tell me that you don't want Rachid. I see the yearning in your eyes whenever we speak of him. You can have it all, Zhang. You can have love and a fulfilling life, but you'll have to fight for it. Fight for this as hard as you fought for your business and you just might find that you can have both. The question you need to ask yourself is if you want my grandson. If you do, put your fears behind you and go get him. The rest will take care of itself."

All I have to do is admit that I want it?

Not for one night.

Not for six months.

Forever.

With Rachid.

I want his passion, his protection—his baby.

I want to say those vows and mean them.

Hadia interrupted her thoughts. "I met one of your friends."

Lil? Abby? It's a pathetically short list.

"Perhaps friend is too strong of a description. She sat with you a few years ago at a weeklong United Nations conference regarding the conditions of women around the world. She was moved by your commitment to help the women in your country. Her name is Caroline Thelemaque."

The name did not immediately bring a face to mind. "I'm sorry, I don't remember her."

Hadia waved at someone who was stepping out of a cab and onto the street. "That's fine, because she's here now."

What are you up to, Hadia?

Zhang stood along with Hadia to greet the woman who entered the café and approached their table. She was average in height, but her beaming smile lit the room around her. Zhang instantly remembered the woman. Who could forget the vibrant Haitian woman whose confidence had matched her boldly feminine business attire? Today, Caroline's clothing was more subdued, but her energy wasn't. Her beautiful black hair, which proudly displayed a few gray highlights, was partially covered in a fashionable scarf, most likely donned out of deference for Hadia.

She bowed slightly before Hadia and warmly shook her hand. "Your Majesty, this invitation is a real honor, thank you." She shook Zhang's hand enthusiastically and said, "Miss Yajun. Princess. I'm not sure how to address you."

Zhang couldn't help but return the woman's warm smile. "Please, call me Zhang."

Hadia sat, and the two younger women joined her.

Hadia said, "Caroline is here with a video team. She's documenting how the focus on education and technology is already changing the conditions of the women in our rural areas. Rachid's passing laws that require young women to stay in school until the age of eighteen. He wants to see more of them studying at our universities."

Zhang sat forward. "I didn't realize that was one of Rachid's goals."

Hadia said, "Perhaps you have more in common than you know."

Uncomfortable with that truth, Zhang directed her comment to Caroline. "The last time I spoke to you, you were living in Canada and raising funds for an empowerment project in Haiti, am I right?"

Caroline ordered a coffee before answering. "Yes, I still am. It is an amazing program. We teach the women the basics of a business and guide them toward the resources needed to support it. For example, making purses from old cereal boxes is a way a woman can create income for her family while recycling what would be trash into something valuable."

Suddenly Zhang regretted that she had not followed up her initial donation to the woman with additional monies. She'd rectify that in the near future. For now, she asked, "Are these videos part of your fund-raising?"

"No, I'm not actually making the videos. I merely joined the team because I had heard so many wonderful things about what is going on here. Sometimes I visit success stories to reenergize. When you look at women's issues on the global level, it can be overwhelming. They aren't contained by borders and aren't specific to cultures. Everywhere I go, I meet women struggling with poverty, abuse or simply the belief that they can't improve their own situation. Places like Najriad are a reminder that we are making progress, but it's never easy."

Hadia added, "Abuse and tradition can sometimes be woven tightly together. It takes a delicate hand to tend to one while not shredding the other. Caroline, I have heard good things about you and how you walk that line." She looked across at Zhang and said, "I believe you do the same with your own programs in China, Zhang."

Zhang nodded. "I still meet resistance at first. Initially, many parents believe that I advocate discarding our ways and adopting those of the West. Over time, they see that education doesn't threaten one's morality. Being able to read doesn't make a young girl promiscuous, but it may help her feed her children if her husband dies young. The belief that the men of your family will care for you only holds true if you have a family. I'm extremely passionate about the power of education to strengthen communities."

Caroline said, "You are an inspiration for women around the world, Zhang, and what you've done for the women's movement in China is what legends are made of. I can only imagine the hope you will bring Najriad when you become queen."

In the face of the woman's compliments and enthusiasm, Zhang felt a bit of a fraud. She almost announced that the likelihood of her becoming involved in local issues was slim. She and Rachid would most likely divorce long before he took the title of king.

Unless I stay.

Zhang's mouth dried and her stomach churned at the thought.

I'm not staying.

Am I?

Impulsively, she asked, "Caroline, are you married?"

The woman flashed a brilliant smile. "Yes. Twenty years."

"And you still travel the world? That's not a problem?"

Caroline seemed to sense the importance of the questions Zhang was asking. "My husband isn't always happy when I leave, but what I am doing is important to me and he knows that."

Oddly, it felt safe to share her inner fear with these women. "I fought for my independence for so long, the idea of marriage scares me. I'm afraid that I'll lose myself somehow."

Hadia smiled sympathetically and Caroline said, "I'm sure I felt the same in the beginning, but my husband knows that he married a strong, independent woman. Sure, it's difficult sometimes, but we work it out. I love him and he knows that. He loves me and he proves it by accepting the good with the bad. I can't always go everywhere I'd like to because he needs me or the children need me. Marriage is a compromise for both involved. Anyone who says that it's always easy is lying, but I've never regretted choosing love."

Zhang couldn't help but be moved by the woman's commitment to both her husband and herself. "It sounds like your husband is a very lucky man."

Caroline's easy smile flashed. "He is. I have given him two

wonderful children: our son, Patrick, and our daughter, Sarah, and we don't fight for who is in control. I understand that he needs to be the man in our house, and he understands that a happy wife is the best nurturer for both him and our children. Marriage doesn't have to be a tug of war. Compromise is a gift you give the man you love and, if he is the right man for you, it is a gift he returns tenfold."

Tears filled Zhang's eyes as she realized that she and her mother had never discussed this topic, and she doubted they ever would. Had these women always been so comfortable with themselves or had someone guided them?

As if sensing Zhang's downward turn in mood, Caroline lightened the conversation by saying, "That about sums up my marital advice, except that you should never underestimate the power of keeping passion alive between you. Many couples push each other aside for the children or for work. A hungry man is never a happy man. Keep your husband well fed and you will have a marriage your friends will envy."

Zhang said, "I don't cook."

Hadia and Caroline exchanged a look and laughed. Hadia said, "My future daughter-in-law has a dry sense of humor. A wise woman is not afraid to please her husband."

Zhang turned three shades of purple.

Caroline rushed to say, "I hope I didn't cross any lines, sharing as I did. I'm not shy when it comes to discussing love and marriage."

Zhang regained her composure and said, "Some of my best friends are oversharers. It's a trait I'm beginning to value." She turned to Hadia and said, "I'm also beginning to admire the fine art of manipulation."

Unabashedly, Hadia accepted the assessment of her actions that day. "You have done so much for your own country, Zhang. I wanted you to see that your work is far from over. Caroline came to meet you today because she admires you, but I wonder if there isn't also much that she could teach you."

Suddenly humble, Caroline said, "Oh, I would never

129

suggest that I —"

Zhang spoke over her and said, "You are one clever lady, Your Majesty. Caroline, would you return for a visit in a few weeks? Perhaps you could stay at the palace. I would love to speak with you more about what you do with your global programs."

"I would be honored to, Your Highness."

For the first time, Zhang didn't baulk at the title. "The honor would be mine," she said.

She smiled at the two women who sat across from her and marveled at the wisdom of the universe.

Two very different women who shared many fundamental beliefs and had found happiness.

Hadia might be right.

I still have so much to learn.

A knock on the door of the palace's main office interrupted Rachid's phone call with his team at Proximus. Rachid put them on hold, turned in the leather seat behind the large desk and said, "Enter," in Arabic.

Basir, the royal advisor, entered and bowed slightly with respect. "Your Highness."

"If you're looking for my father, he and Ghalil have gone out for the morning. They should be back for dinner."

"My apologies for interrupting, Your Highness, but it's you I wish to speak with," the old man said.

"One moment, then." Rachid switched to English to inform his team that he would continue the call at a later time and issued a short list of what he wanted done before they spoke again. "Please, sit," he said to the royal advisor, not realizing that he continued to speak in English. Another tap on the door announced the delivery of a pot of coffee. The house staff maintained proper etiquette, smoothly covering for Rachid's shortcomings. Rachid refused the beverage, but Basir took one of the small, handleless cups the manservant offered, sipped from it and smiled at the servant, who quickly departed.

As soon as the door closed behind him, Basir said, "There was a second attempt on your father's life this morning. His private motorcade took gunfire."

The first attempt had occurred shortly after the announcement that Rachid was returning home. Security had been increased in all areas. A second attack was upsetting, but expected since the attacker had not been caught the first time. "Was anyone hurt?" Rachid said, standing and crossing to where the advisor sat.

"No, it was a decoy. Your father and brother are safely visiting with Sheikh Hamad bin Dani al Butrus at the palace in Sasiah."

"Does my father know?"

"Not yet, but his security has been informed. Protective measures will be taken on their return. The fewer who know about this, the better."

"Who did this?" Rachid paced the room angrily.

Basir lifted a thin shoulder and said, "Some are saying that it was our people protesting against your upcoming marriage to a foreign woman."

Rachid stopped midstep. That would be an unfortunate complication. Basir, however, hadn't sounded convinced. "But you don't think so?"

"I have no proof, but my instincts tell me that this is being used as a smokescreen to distract us from something much more sinister that's being set into plan. I know the leaders of the communities well, and there was no buildup to this." He gave Rachid a long, steady look. "Also, I find it suspicious that neither attack put your father's life at risk."

"What are you saying, Basir? Someone is trying to make it look like my father's life is in danger without it actually being so? Why would anyone do that?" The answer came to Rachid before the advisor said a word. "To discredit me."

Basir inclined his head. "Exactly. This enemy is more dangerous than the ones who test our borders. This is a snake hidden in the grass—not bold enough to attack you yet, but just as deadly."

"Do we have any leads?"

"Only that whoever it is, they know where your father won't be. You must consider everyone." He paused, then said, "Even Ghalil."

"No," Rachid said hotly. It was one thing to admit that Ghalil was angry and distrustful, but a traitor? He wouldn't believe it. "My brother is not involved in this."

Basir wisely lowered his eyes respectfully as he said, "History is littered with stories of dead royals who thought the same."

Rachid said, "I know my brother. He's young and he often speaks without thinking, but he wouldn't do something like this."

"I hope your faith in him does not prove to be your undoing."

I hope so, too.

There was another possibility.

"Basir, it could be a member of the royal guard." His next words were the toughest to voice. "They aren't loyal to me."

Basir made no attempt to deny the truth. He said, "It is a sign of real strength to be able to admit a weakness."

Rachid pounded an angry hand on the wall. "This particular weakness may get us all killed. How can I run a financial empire outside Najriad—one where my orders are followed without question—but here in my own country I must repeat myself and add a threat for anything to happen?"

Basir said, "It sounds like you understand what motivates one more than the other."

Rachid sighed. "Sometimes I ask myself if I'm the right man to rule Najriad."

Basir said, "Perhaps you are not." Rachid's head swung around in shock. Plain speaking was what made Basir a valuable asset to the Hantan family, but that didn't remove the sting from his words. Basir added, "Not as long as you ask yourself that.

What makes a good king, Rachid?" When Rachid didn't answer, Basir asked, "Why do the people love your father?"

"My father has devoted his life to Najriad."

"Yes, he sacrificed many things along the way—even his first son." Rachid turned and simply absorbed Basir's words. "He gave you to the world because he knew you would come back and do what he was unable to—break our dependency on natural resources. He didn't make the decision easily, but he did it. The royal guard protects him because he protects all of us. If you wish for a man to be willing to give his life for you, you must first ask yourself if you are willing to give yours for him."

Rachid growled, "I am."

"Then prove it, Your Highness, and the people will follow you."

"How am I supposed to do that?"

Basir bowed his head. "Only you can answer that question, Your Highness."

Rachid turned his back on the advisor and stared out the window.

Accepting his dismissal, Basir opened the door and said quietly, "Find comfort, young prince, in the knowledge that your father once asked me the same question and I gave him the same answer."

Chapter Thirteen

Later that day, Zhang paced the rooms of her palace suite like a caged lioness.

Hadia's words haunted her. *"You can have love and a fulfilling life, but you'll have to fight for it. Fight for this as hard as you fought for your business and you just might find that you can have both."*

I'm not afraid to fight for what I want.

But is this what I want?

Rachid was chauvinistic and arrogant, but he was also tender and strong. Yes, he had locked her in like she was a purchased addition to a harem, but he'd done it to protect her. If Hadia spoke the truth, he'd stood up to his father to defend her and had given her honor more importance than his freedom.

In the middle of a battle for the sovereignty of his country and for his right to rule it, he had chosen to protect her. No, he didn't see her as his equal yet. If he did, he would open up to her and she would hear of his troubles from him rather than his grandmother. But he was a good man who cared about her and wanted her with the same intensity that she wanted him.

I can work with that. Zhang used Rachid's own words and smiled.

"You're mine," he'd said in his passionate, possessive manner.

I can work with that, too, she thought, *as long as it goes both ways.*

She considered calling Rachid to tell him that she'd changed her mind. They wouldn't have time alone once the guests arrived. As it was, now that she'd agreed to the wedding, their time together was frowned upon. According to the customs of Najriad, Zhang was supposed to retreat into a period of reflection and preparation. The next time she was scheduled to see Rachid was when her parents met the king and they signed the wedding contract.

I don't know if I can wait that long. What if he doesn't come to me before then?

He'll think I'm crazy if I demand to see him now just to tell him that I want to marry him—even though we're already getting married. You don't tell a man that your independence is the only thing you care about one day and say the exact opposite the next day.

A marriage can't be ordered as if from a menu.

Did I say temporary with a side of get me the hell out of here?

I meant forever with a splash of happily ever after.

Panic flooded Zhang and she sat heavily on the edge of her bed, clasping her shaking hands on her lap.

I've lost my mind.

Or your heart, the universe whispered.

Or my heart, Zhang repeated in agreement.

She let herself imagine a life in Najriad with Rachid. She'd help him bring the headquarters of Proximus to Nilon. Together they could work to increase opportunities for the rural families who lived in poverty—men and women. With Hadia's advice, she would learn how to navigate the local customs.

Hadia. Zhang smiled when she thought about the woman she would never underestimate again.

Grandmother.

My grandmother if I choose this life.

And I do.

Rachid is a good man and we can work together to make a strong marriage—one in which love will take root and flourish. A life that isn't about my goals or his goals, but about our shared vision for both.

Her heart soared as her indecision fell away and she knew exactly what she wanted to do with the rest of her life.

Regardless of what I've said, on Saturday I will make this solemn vow: Rachid bin Amir al Hantan—I will give you forever.

On the other side of the palace, Rachid paced the rooms of his suite like a caged lion.

I can't even protect my own family—why did I think I could protect Zhang?

His first instinct was to cancel the wedding. However, it was too late to change course. Zhang's family would be dealt a public embarrassment if the wedding didn't happen, and appearing indecisive would only help his enemies make their case against him.

He should call his American friends and tell them not to come, but changing plans in response to the recent attack would be taken as weakness. Nothing is more dangerous than showing your enemy that you're vulnerable.

I should have never asked her to marry me. I should have found another way, but once again satisfying my own needs has put someone I care about in danger.

Yes, on some level the decision had been to restore her honor, but Rachid was battling the disturbing knowledge that it had also stemmed from a much less noble truth. *I wanted her. I didn't care that she was afraid of what it would do to the life she'd built. I didn't care enough about her to look for another solution. I laid claim to her and in my arrogance I thought we could build a future on that shaky foundation.*

I let lust drive my actions, and the result is that a good woman must pay the price for my mistakes. Possibly with her life, if I don't find the traitor in my household.

He sat heavily on the edge of his bed, one that he'd told her they'd soon share, and knew what he had to do.

She was right to ask to keep the marriage short.

I can't go back in time and undo what we've done.

I can't guarantee that she won't regret her time here, but I can give her what she wants more than anything else.

On Saturday, regardless of what I say aloud, I will make this solemn vow: Zhang Yajun—I will set you free.

Chapter Fourteen

To Zhang's surprise, the next morning Rachid sent for her to join him in the castle office. He remained planted in the middle of the room as she entered, his hands clasped behind him. He was still dressed in a simple white thobe and keffiyeh, but there was something different about him. "Come in," he said.

She walked directly up to him, hoping he liked the black gown she'd chosen with him in mind, and deliberately placed herself within his reach. His features remained set in harsh lines, far from the reaction she was hoping for. His mood was so distinctly different from any of their other times together that Zhang asked, "Has something happened?"

"No," he answered. "However, we marry tomorrow and there are things we need to discuss."

You have that right!

If this is where you remind me that despite what I said about wanting to keep our marriage platonic, we are going to share the same bed—I'm okay with that now. You don't even have to say you love me, just give me some indication that Hadia is right and you do care for me.

He cleared his throat. "I made sure that part of the marriage contract clearly states that I will have no access to your company or your money, regardless of how long our marriage lasts. Also, after Sunday, you will be free to go back and forth to China as you need to."

"Thank you," Zhang said as her stomach twisted painfully.

"Consider this office at your disposal for now. You don't need an escort to move around the palace, but you may want to request one until you learn the layout. If you'd prefer, I can have an office set up near your rooms."

My rooms? What about our rooms? "That's very kind of you," she said slowly. "Either will be fine."

Zhang couldn't interpret the look in Rachid's eyes. She reached out a hand to touch his chest, but he took a step back. Her hand dropped to her side. *Okay. Now I'm concerned.*

He said, "How did you enjoy your tour of Nilon with my grandmother?"

"I enjoyed the tour immensely and your grandmother is an incredible woman." She wanted to say more but sensed that he wasn't finished speaking. How had they gone from whispering their secret desires to each other to speaking like acquaintances making light conversation? She wanted to grab him by the shoulders and shake him until he told her what was going on.

Rachid continued his polite discourse. "It's good that you get along. She can help you prepare whatever you need for the ceremony. Guests have already started to arrive. My grandmother said that you have a small party planned for tonight."

"Yes," Zhang said, "henna for the women."

Talk to me, Rachid. Although he was looking at her, her fiancé felt a million miles away.

Rachid nodded. "My grandmother will enjoy that."

Luckily it wasn't going to be a wild party.

Rachid said, "You understand what will happen on Saturday? We will make our vows before my father in the meeting room, in front of your parents. They will exchange presents. We will sign papers. There will be a short interval." He looked uncomfortable for a moment. "Traditionally, this was when the bride and groom would consummate their vows and then return to share a meal with their new families. More often the time is now used to take photos, but neither will be necessary for us."

Not even the consummation?

Where is the prince with the wandering hands and the hot kisses? I was hoping to spend the rest of my life with him.

139

"I suppose not," Zhang said abruptly.

"I know this hasn't been easy on you, Zhang," Rachid said and touched her cheek lightly, then pulled his hand back as if he hadn't meant to do it and quickly regretted the action. "But I will make it right. I promise you that." His eyes filled with a sadness that sent a panic cutting through her. "Tomorrow evening we will gather in the main dining hall for a shared meal. Sunday, the celebration will continue or we can send the guests home. Whichever you'd like."

Zhang stepped toward him. *I'd like you to tell me what the hell is wrong.*

He turned away from her and headed toward the door.

"Rachid," Zhang said, his name torn from her.

He looked back, concerned by the urgency in her voice. "Yes?"

"Are you sure nothing has happened?"

His lips thinned. "Nothing I can't handle."

Alone.

He didn't need to say the word out loud—Zhang knew what he meant. Still, she had to try to reach him. "No matter what it is, I can help."

A slight smile pursed his lips. "You are an amazing woman, Zhang, and your offer is generous, but this is something I have to do. "

He closed the door behind him, leaving her standing in the middle of the office.

It would be easy to let insecurity sweep in. Easy to convince herself that he had changed his mind and didn't want her anymore.

Insecurity, like indecision, was an unproductive weakness that she deliberately denied herself. A man couldn't fake the kind of desire he'd had for her and that didn't disappear overnight. Something had happened.

Something big.

I can let whatever it is determine my destiny, or I can fight for what I want.

And I've always enjoyed a good fight.

Do you hear me, Universe?

Rachid is mine.

Now all I need to do is find out what is standing in our way.

Zhang crossed the room and sat in the leather chair behind the desk. A quick search of the drawers produced nothing she could read. Sitting back, her eyes settled on the computer **on** the corner of the desk and an idea came to her.

Rachid, I'm glad you didn't have me promise to stay out of your business.

I hate lying.

Dialing the number of a man she'd once thought of only as a way to fund one of her programs in China, Zhang reflected on the unexpected turns life could take. She'd never been one to ask anyone for help, but her instincts told her that whatever was going on with Rachid was important enough to put her pride aside. Speaking to the man who answered the phone, she said, "Dominic, I need a favor."

Like a man asked to move a couch for the third time, Dominic sighed and said, "Don't tell me, now you want to leave."

Zhang said, "No. I'm staying. I just need to borrow one of your employees."

"Mrs. Duhamel? She's already busy watching Colby for Lil."

"Why would I want your personal assistant?"

"I don't know, to plan one of those beauty days or something. Don't women like to get made over for their wedding day?"

Feminine pride kicked in. Zhang frowned and asked, "What are you trying to say, Dominic?"

Wising up, Dominic hastily added, "Why don't you tell me what you need."

Zhang bit back a smile. Abby was training him well. "Didn't you recently hire a hacker?"

"And if I did?"

"Have him fly over tonight. And tell him to pack translation software. He's going to need it."

"What's going on, Zhang?"

"Something's not right here. I have a feeling that Rachid is in danger."

Dominic cursed and said, "Are you sure you don't simply want to get the hell out? Say the word and we'll make it happen."

And he would.

Zhang wasn't the type of person to hug anyone, but had Dominic been in the same room with her, she might have made an exception in his case. Like her, he'd fought for everything he had and it'd given him a tough exterior.

They were both discovering the same lesson: No one spent their last moments of life tallying the worth of their possessions. What mattered in the end was if you loved and were loved—and how that experience shaped your actions.

Dominic was a better person since he'd met his new wife.

I want that. "Rachid and I will marry tomorrow, Dom. We're going to have a long and happy life together." *I'm willing to risk everything for a chance at that.*

Dominic said, "Not if Rachid discovers what you're up to."

Zhang tapped her nails impatiently on the back of the phone. "Your concern is touching, Dominic, but I just need to know if you're in."

"Let's see. Extremely covert, highly illegal, potentially explosive—do you really have to ask? Of course I'm in." He was quiet for a moment. "Jeremy is working with an image consultant. I'll tell him that attending this wedding is part of his education. He may have to bring a date, though."

"That's fine. The more people who come, the better. We'll need the distraction to make this work. Do you think we should involve Jake?"

"No, he'd never go for this. Trust me, it's easier to ask for forgiveness than permission."

Zhang released a breath she'd unconsciously been holding. "Dominic, I'll owe you for this."

Dominic said, "No, you won't. You're a good friend to my wife. That goes a long way with me." He cleared his throat and said, "I'd like to see you happy, Zhang."

His words made Zhang want to laugh and cry at the same time. "Me too," she said softly and hung up.

Me too.

Rachid met with the head of the Royal Guardsmen, Marshid. "The house will be full of guests this weekend and the family will be focused on the festivities."

"Yes, Your Highness."

"I want extra security on my father. Two guards at all times and I want them rotated. All of our resources will be directed toward protecting the rest of the royal family and our guests. I will also need you to relax the security around me. For this to work, I will require times when I am unprotected."

Marshid frowned in question. "Sir?"

"There is a traitor among us and I am going to draw him out. I'll announce at the wedding that I'm moving up the date of my coronation. That news, with the cover of the wedding, should provide enough of an opportunity for someone to take action if they are going to. Trust no one."

"Are you suggesting it could be one of the Royal Guardsmen?" the man was offended.

"I don't know who it is, but I'm betting my life that we can figure it out in time."

"That's a dangerous plan, sir."

"Someone is threatening my family and they're doing it from inside the palace. They could easily slay us all while we sleep. This way, the only life that's risked is mine. Just make sure that if I die, you catch the bastard who did it."

Marshid stood taller and looked Rachid directly in the eyes. "Yes, Your Highness."

Zhang was navigating the maze of hallways that led back to the women's quarters when Rachid's younger brother, Ghalil, appeared. He was walking in the other direction and looked like he might pass her without so much as a nod of acknowledgement, but at the last moment he stopped and glared down at her. "Your audacity amazes me."

Zhang kept her expression polite. "Does it?" she asked blandly.

"Yes, I find it amazing that you are willing to marry my brother when it is obvious that the people of Najriad don't want you. You should leave before someone gets hurt."

Magma-like fury that had been building finally found an outlet. Had Ghalil known Zhang better he would have backed away from her small smile and soft tone—both indicators of a deadly calm before a storm. "I find your complete lack of loyalty to your brother equally amazing, and only a coward confronts a woman when he thinks she's alone and vulnerable." Ghalil opened his mouth to say something but Zhang leaned closer and snarled, "Your mistake is that I'm not vulnerable, and if you'd like to test the truth of my words lay a hand on me and see how long you keep it. I don't require the protection of your guardsmen, but you may if you're not careful."

"You dare to threaten me?" Ghalil's voice rose with anger. "I could have you thrown in prison."

Zhang's lips curled derisively. "I'd love to see you try. Go tell your father that when you attempted to scare one of the women under his protection, she didn't cower like you'd hoped. I'm sure he'll take that news well. Or better yet, complain to Rachid if you're feeling brave today."

Shaking with anger, Zhang didn't notice the head of the Royal Guardsmen approach until he spoke behind Ghalil. "Are you lost, Miss Yajun? Would you like me to escort you anywhere?"

His expression revealed he'd heard at least part of the

conversation and didn't approve of how the young prince was behaving. Zhang nodded and gracefully accepted his offer of assistance. The flush on Ghalil's face hinted that he had more to say, and Zhang was positive she didn't want to hear it. "I was returning to my room," she answered.

She walked beside the guard down the hallway and into an area of the palace Ghalil would never follow. At her door, she let out a shaky breath and said, "Thank you."

The guard bowed slightly.

Before opening the door behind her, Zhang asked, "Is he right? Are the people unhappy with me?"

The man answered slowly, seeming to choose his words with care. "They don't know you, but you will have time to rectify that."

"Will I?" Zhang asked. "I get the feeling that there is more than a wedding going on at the palace this weekend."

"Your safety isn't threatened," the guard answered obliquely.

"I'm not worried about me. I have resources, even locally, that could be useful if I knew what was going on."

The guard didn't blink.

Zhang said, "You're not going to tell me anything, are you?" When he still said nothing, Zhang added, "I appreciate your loyalty, but you need to know one thing."

He met her eyes.

"If Rachid is in danger, I'll do whatever it takes to protect him. Don't stand in my way."

A glimmer of approval shone in what was otherwise a carefully expressionless face. With a completely noncommittal bow, the guard excused himself.

Rachid, what kind of trouble are you in?

When I said I'd fight for you, I was speaking figuratively.

I really have to watch how I phrase things.

Why do fairy tales always make it look easy?

All Snow White had to do was take a long nap.

I'm probably going to get killed trying to save my prince.

Unexpected humor tickled her as Zhang entered her suite and slid off her shoes.

There's my next career if this doesn't work out—children's books.

Fairy Tales From the Edge, by Princess Zhang bin Amir al Hantan.

Each book would come with one of those adorable, elaborately dressed dolls, but when a child pulled the string coming out of its back, instead of spouting sweet phrases it would say, "Don't fuck with my happy ending."

Chapter Fifteen

That evening, Zhang served tea to her mother in the lavish sitting room of the suite the king had designated for her parents. Her mother was dressed in formfitting long-sleeved rose qipao. The collar was buttoned and embroidered with blue flowers. The silk dress was accented beautifully by an embroidered sash that crossed the bodice at an angle.

Conversation hadn't come easily to the two women since Zhang had left Xin. In Mandarin, Zhang asked, "Do you have everything you need?"

Her mother made a delicately displeased face and said, "The tea is British. You should have warned me."

Zhang breathed a sigh of relief. Her mother had chosen a safe topic. Her criticisms were harmless in general. Zhang doubted her mother knew how to give a compliment. Critiquing the choice of tea was practically an olive branch as far as Zhang was concerned. "I'll have one of the staff locate some green tea. I'm sure they have it."

Her mother took another sip. "I met the king. He seemed pleasant. A bit fat."

Zhang bit her lip to conceal the smile that almost spread across her face. Sometimes it was not a bad thing that her mother refused to learn English.

"Your father told me that we will be attending a henna party." A hint of distaste flitted across her face. "Isn't that when people put temporary tattoos on? I hope your friends don't have an allergic reaction to it."

Zhang choked on her tea. Her mother was planning on being there? "I didn't think you'd want to attend the party today. I thought you'd want to rest."

Her mother's eyes burned into hers. "I was told all female members of the family were invited. Rachid's grandmother is attending. Do you not want me there?"

Why do I always feel like I'm navigating a minefield when I talk to her?

"Of course I want you there."

Liar, liar. . .

Putting her cup down, her mother said, "Tomorrow you join your husband's family. I used to think that was the saddest part of having a daughter." When Zhang started to say something, her mother smoothed the skirt of her dress and said, "It's not."

Oh, boy, here it comes.

"Sad is when you lose your daughter before marriage." Her mother drove her words home by meeting her daughter's eyes as she said, "I do hope you enjoy your new family more than you did ours."

Instant tears clogged Zhang's throat. "Mother..."

Chin held high with pride, her mother said, "Please don't deny it, Zhang. I was never the mother you wanted. Never good enough for you. If it weren't for your father, I doubt you would have included me in this weekend at all."

Zhang couldn't deny the truth in her mother's accusation, although it wasn't because she didn't think her mother was good enough. Quite the reverse. She sought a conciliatory approach. "Father says we are too much alike to get along."

A delicate, skeptical eyebrow rose on her mother's face.

Zhang added, "I'm stubborn to a fault."

Her mother agreed. "And outspoken to the point of rudeness."

Zhang continued, "I could pick a fight with Ghandi."

Her mother smiled ever so faintly and said, "You could."

Zhang grinned. "And win."

Her mother shook her head in disapproval but said, "You probably would."

Zhang deliberately added, "You'd do the same."

For just a heartbeat their differences faded into the background. "I might."

Zhang stopped herself from reaching out to touch her mother as she said, "I know I'm not the daughter you wanted, but you're wrong about some things. You were a very good mother and I wanted to want the things you did. If I could have, I would have stayed with Xin and made you proud of me, but I needed something else."

"Something better?" Although the question was issued in a harsh tone, Zhang heard the hurt.

"No." Leaning forward, Zhang willed her mother to understand. "Just different."

Neither woman spoke for a moment. Then her mother gestured to the room with one hand and said, "Well, this place is certainly different. Your prince is a handsome man, for a foreigner."

Zhang nodded.

Her mother stood. "Let's go to this henna party. My hands could do with some decoration."

Amazed and feeling somewhat hopeful, Zhang asked, "You're going to let someone tattoo you?"

Completely straight-faced, her mother asked, "You think you're the only one with a wild side?"

Zhang laughed until a lone tear ran down her face. She joined her mother near the door and said, "I pick and choose which traditions I follow. Tomorrow, I'll join Rachid's family, but only on the condition that you and Father are welcome to live here as well. We may have our issues, but you never lost me and you never will."

Her mother waited for Zhang to open the door for her and countered, "We? I don't have issues," but there was a twinkle in her eyes that Zhang hadn't seen in many, many years.

Zhang bowed respectfully, smiling at the floor. "Of course not, Mother."

As they stepped into the hallway, her mother asked, "Are you sure you want to wear that dress tonight?"

Zhang looked down at the green silk qipao that Hadia had given her for the evening. It was less ornate than her mother's but was an exquisitely made piece of Chinese formal wear. She knew her mother loved her choice and therefore wasn't bothered by her question. There was relief in returning to normal. Parts of their relationship would always be comfortably uncomfortable.

And that's okay.

On the first floor of the palace, Rachid's bachelor party was underway. Despite the Egyptian pop musician that played in the background and the smoke haze of the Behike cigars the men were smoking, the mood remained relatively serious. King Amir and Zhang's father had retired to another room, claiming they didn't want to slow the younger men down. Since alcohol and female dancers were not an option, Rachid doubted there would be very much difference between the level of excitement with or without the two fathers.

Rachid asked, "Dominic, how does it look for China next week?"

Dominic took a puff of his cigar and studied his old friend before answering. "Everything is on schedule." Another puff and he asked casually, "I'd rather discuss why you decided to partner with Andrade Solutions when you needed an innovative product for Proximus."

Jeremy, the man Dominic had requested attend the wedding for "socialization" purposes, entered the conversation with complete disregard for the tension in Dominic's voice. "Andrade Solutions is cutting-edge. They are designing atomic-scale wires that will blow the roof off of how many transistors can be squeezed onto an integrated circuit. That's going to seriously shrink the size of supercomputers."

Jake sat forward in his chair and said, "You never cease to amaze me, Jeremy."

Even Rachid wasn't sure if Jake was complimenting or insulting the hacker, but Jeremy shrugged and heard what he wanted to. "Because I can read? It's all over the Internet. I'm dying for quantum computers to become a viable option for the public. In fact, I wish they'd take the patents out of the hands of physicists and give them to game developers—the technology would be in the market already instead of stashed away at university labs. I want holographic screens, expression recognition, and I want them in something the size of my phone."

In the pause that followed, Rachid realized Dominic was ignoring Jeremy's enthusiastic endorsement of Stephan's latest projects and was waiting for Rachid's answer. He said, "Dom, I would have approached you at your wedding, but it wasn't the best place to talk business. I haven't signed a contract with Stephan. We are merely talking."

"I don't give a damn about the business side of this, Rachid. If you need something, you come to me," Dominic said in a tone that brought an uncomfortable stillness to the room.

As generous as the offer was, even Dominic couldn't fix this situation. "I appreciate that, Dom."

"I'm serious, Rachid. At the end of the day, we've been friends for more than ten years. You can ask me for anything." He ground out what was left of his cigar on the tray next to him. "Unless I'm on my postponed honeymoon. If anyone calls me that week, they had better be gasping their last breath."

Curious, Jeremy latched on to what he found fascinating. "How did you all meet?"

Grateful for the change of subject, Rachid said, "I believe I stumbled upon Jake trying to stop a rugby team from beating the life out of Dominic."

Jake smiled. "I almost forgot that's how we met."

Dominic countered, "I was fine. It wasn't the whole team."

Rachid shared what he remembered. "Only about eight of them. Huge, hairy guys. Two of them were holding Dom while another punched. What did you do to deserve that beating?"

Leaning back in his chair, Dominic shrugged. "I don't even remember now."

Jake laughed. "I do. You told one of them that when you'd left their mother that morning she hadn't mentioned how ugly her son was. Or something like that."

Dominic grinned. "Oh, yeah. Trust me, that was nothing compared to what he'd said to me about mine. I may have miscalculated how angry they would all be when I retaliated."

Jake leaned toward Jeremy as if he were sharing confidential information. "Dominic used to have a bit of an attitude problem."

Shaking his head in amusement, Dominic denied the accusation. "I was working to pay my way through college. I didn't have the energy for an attitude. You were the one living comfortably off Mom and Dad's money. You should have jumped in and saved me."

"I did. I convinced them that if it took that many of them to take you down, they should consider asking you to join their team," Jake said.

Dominic groaned. "So, I have you to thank for the following two years of broken noses and fractures."

Jake pointed to Rachid. "You can also blame him. They were his teammates."

Rachid put both hands up and laughed. "Hey, by the time I came on the scene it was mostly over, and Jake sounded like he was negotiating a professional career contract for you with the captain. All I did was agree that you should join the team."

Shrugging, Jake said, "It was good for you, Dom. You needed an outlet for all that anger." Moving on to another topic, he said, "I wonder what the women are up to today."

Rachid thought about the mix of women and said, "Probably not that much. My grandmother and Zhang's mother joined them. How much fun could they be having?"

With a certain level of apprehension, Zhang led her mother into the main rooms of the women's quarters, where she knew her friends were already gathered. The room was at least four times the size of her own sitting room and split into several sections, designated by clusters of modern leisure furniture and rugs topped with pillows likely also meant as seating. All of the women stood when she entered.

Hadia approached and greeted her with several cheek kisses. Zhang stopped counting after the third. When the older woman looked behind her and saw her mother, her face lit up with real joy. She stopped short of touching her.

Xiaoli politely looked down in greeting while instructing her daughter in Mandarin, "Don't let that woman touch me."

Hadia looked to Zhang for a translation. In English, Zhang lied. "She said that it's an honor to meet you."

Hadia smiled and ushered them both in.

Abby and Lil stepped forward together to greet Zhang. Abby gave her a short hug and said, "You look so beautiful, Zhang!"

Zhang blushed.

Lil crushed Zhang to her in a much more exuberant embrace. "This palace is fantastic, isn't it? You must love it here. Just exotic enough to feel like you're in another country without having to wonder how to use the toilets."

Leave it Lil to put everything in perspective.

Zhang smiled and hugged her friend. She stepped back and introduced them to her mother. "Abby, Lil, this is my mother Yajun Xiaoli. You may call her Mrs. Yajun. Please excuse the fact that she doesn't speak English."

Xiaoli smiled politely at the two women and said, "These are the women you told me about? I imagined them more beautiful."

Under her breath, Zhang said, "Stop, Mother."

Abby cut into the conversation with an easy smile and, without noting that she'd understood Xiaoli's comment, used some of the little Mandarin she knew. "Mrs. Yajun, nice to meet you."

Zhang held back her amusement when her mother's jaw dropped. Xiaoli slowly recovered her composure and returned the greeting. With a tight smile, she said, "My daughter didn't mention that you spoke Mandarin."

A born peacemaker, Abby said, "My vocabulary is quite limited, but you are welcome to sit beside me tonight if you'd like someone to speak with."

Somewhat chastised, her mother thanked Abby but refused to meet her daughter's eyes. Which was probably a good thing because Zhang wasn't sure she could have kept a straight face.

Lil bowed her head in greeting to Zhang's mother but addressed her sister as she did. "Abby, you are so lucky to know as many languages as you do."

Abby smiled at Zhang and said, "It has plusses and minuses."

In that small joke, Zhang was reminded of one of the many reasons she loved these women. Abby could have taken her mother's comment to heart and been offended. Instead, she found humor in the situation and therefore made the entire evening more bearable. No matter what happened, they could laugh about this later.

A final woman stepped forward, and Zhang guessed that she must be the infamous image consultant of Dominic's new hacker. Although Jeremy Kater was touted to be brilliant with computers, Zhang's one encounter with him had left her with the impression that he had not spent much time outside his basement. She didn't envy this woman's job. Zhang extended a hand and said, "You must be Jeisa Borreto. I'm pleased you could join us."

The beautiful Brazilian woman stepped forward and took Zhang's hand warmly in hers. "The pleasure is mine. I hope I'm not intruding on this special occasion. I didn't want to not attend since I was invited, but I see now that this is a very private affair and I should probably retire back to my room."

Lil interjected, "You can't miss this, Jeisa."

Zhang held the woman's hand a moment longer and said, "I would be honored if you stayed and joined us."

With that, all the women moved to sit on one side of the

room. An uncomfortable silence fell over the group as no one was quite sure what to say.

Hadia asked Jeisa, "Where are you from?"

With a light Portuguese accent, the golden-skinned beauty said, "Santo Amaro. Have you been there, Your Majesty?"

Hadia shook her head and said, "Regretfully, no, but I have heard it called the Manhattan of Brazil, so I imagine it is quite crowded and full of fashion."

Jeisa smiled in approval and said, "I believe they would accept that description."

As that topic concluded, another awkward lull stretched on. Zhang looked down at the watch on her wrist. *Where the hell is the henna artist? I thought she'd be here by now.*

A servant entered with a tray of fruits, dips and a variety of breads. Hadia was the first to be served, then Zhang and the other guests. The women sampled the foods quietly. Just as Zhang was ready to label the evening as one of the longest and most painful in recent memory, Lil stood and said, "I have a surprise for you that might liven up this party. Zhang, may I?"

Xiaoli murmured, "I hope she didn't bring a stripper."

Abby concurred in Mandarin, "Me too."

The two women exchanged a quick look, then returned their attention to the bubbly brunette who was setting up a small radio in the corner of the room.

When Zhang didn't call the surprise to a halt, Lil took that as permission to steamroll ahead. Almost instantly, the room filled slow and sensuous Egyptian music. The playful tempo was undeniably captivating. Lil rushed to a pile of boxes she had set nearby and began to hand them out. "I picked these up at a party store, so they aren't authentic or anything, but I'm glad that I purchased extra so everyone can have one."

Lil bowed and gave Hadia her box. "Your Majesty, I hope you don't find this offensive."

Not that that would stop Lil. Zhang smiled and gracefully accepted her own large gift box.

When all the boxes were passed out Zhang realized that

everyone was waiting for her to open hers first. She did and lifted up what looked like a green bikini top adorned with gold chains and medallions for everyone to see.

Lil added hastily, "In the box, there is also a gold-coin belt for everyone. Those are real. I thought they would make a nice memento of this weekend."

As the women opened their boxes and touched the gaudy harem outfits, each more fanciful than the last, Zhang found herself honestly speechless. It was one of those moments where time suspends and you wrestle with a thousand different conflicting reactions.

Abby spoke first, her embarrassment painfully obvious. "Oh, Lil."

Lil defended her gift, not fully reading the mood of the women around her. "It's perfectly appropriate, Abby. I read up about Najriadian customs and how the henna party is all about the women dancing and celebrating. There were several mentions of improvisational belly dancing being popular. I thought this would be fun." She looked around and took in the lack of enthusiasm and turned her question to Zhang. "You're not embarrassed, are you, Zhang? This could be fun, couldn't it?"

Zhang looked at her mother but couldn't read the older woman's expression. She turned to Hadia and was surprised to see her smiling.

Hadia said, "There was dancing at my henna party and music very similar to what you chose, Lil." Her smile widened. "I can't say that I ever wore anything like this, but I can see how it would be—as you say—fun."

Hesitation fell away and Lil said, "So you could show us some traditional dance moves?" She moved her hands in a stiff impression of a Hawaiian dancer.

Only Lil would ask the mother of a king to provide dance lessons.

Zhang held her breath.

Hadia stood and secured the gold-coin belt around her

waist. "I believe I could." She looked down at Zhang's mother, who had not yet opened her box. "I would wear the attire you provided, but by my age some things are best covered." She turned to Zhang. "Your mother, however, is quite youthful. I'll demonstrate some traditional moves, if she will adorn herself with the outfit Lil purchased for her."

Mouth dry and quickly losing an inner battle to hide her shock, Zhang translated the dare to her mother. Fully expecting her mother to issue a haughty refusal, Zhang was stunned when Xiaoli opened her box, carefully inspected each article it contained and smiled slowly.

Xiaoli started to say, "Tell the —" Then she hesitated and glanced at Abby before responding to Zhang with more care. "Tell your new grandmother that I also used to dance and that I would be honored to learn from her." She stood and said, "Please direct me to a changing room."

Zhang pointed to a powder room across the room, then watched her mother walk away with her head held high and Lil's present tucked under her arm. Zhang met Hadia's twinkling eyes and whispered, "I can't believe she's doing it."

Hadia smiled and said, "Lil told me of the dare that brought you and my grandson together." Before Zhang had a chance to be embarrassed, she continued, "I wondered where you got your spunk from. Now I see." She turned to the rest of the women in the room and said, "Of course, you should honor Lil's gifts by wearing them this evening. Zhang's mother cannot be the only woman here who is brave enough to do it."

Zhang whispered to her soon-to-be grandmother, "You are so bad."

Hadia answered with more emotion than Zhang expected her to. "Life is short, Zhang. It is meant to be embraced fully. There will be plenty of reasons to be serious tomorrow. Let yourself enjoy tonight. We gather without the men for a reason. There is no one here to tell us what is or isn't appropriate." She raised her arms gracefully above her head and wiggled her hips from side to side. "Tonight we dance."

When Xiaoli returned from the bathroom, Zhang was stunned at how beautiful her mother looked. Her slim form was accentuated by the costume's small top, and its white sequined harem pants both revealed her flat stomach and flashed her legs as she walked. Although her mother and Hadia spoke different languages, in that moment, they understood each other perfectly.

Two women, beyond the age where many considered themselves attractive, demonstrated that they were both still sensual and vital. Hadia began to move her hips in an angular, repetitive motion that Xiaoli mirrored with ease. The image of the women together was so striking that at first no one moved from their seats. What started as two very separate styles met somewhere in the middle as Hadia adapted some moves to reflect how Xiaoli held herself, and Xiaoli became as fluid and free as the music.

Lil came to stand beside Zhang and said, "Your father may thank me for this later."

No, no, no. Zhang groaned. *You're killing what was a hot fantasy and potentially scarring me for life.*

Lil took Zhang by the hand and said, "Come on, we can't let them have all the fun."

There was a knock on the outside door and a servant entered, followed by a henna artist.

Something about the comical expression of surprise on the artist's face made Zhang laugh. Once she started she couldn't stop, and suddenly she didn't care how this evening looked to an outsider. Hadia was right.

I need to relax and enjoy the good times.

And there is no way that my mother is going to out-dance me at my own bachelorette party.

Zhang leaned down, picked up the box that held her own green, somewhat transparent costume and asked, "Lil, how did you ever think of this?"

Lil glanced over her shoulder at the friend she was dragging behind her and said, "I knew you were worried about tomorrow. I wanted to make you laugh."

Zhang squeezed her young friend's hand. *Goal achieved.* She'd actually forgotten to worry about Rachid's emotional withdrawal, Ghalil's recent threat and the very dangerous risk she was going to take while everyone else enjoyed dinner the next day. Even if it didn't last, Lil had provided her with enough of a distraction that she'd forgotten everything else and, for just a few moments, had simply been a nervous bride.

Lil started shedding her clothing as soon as she reached the powder room, so Zhang hastily closed the door between them. Zhang turned when she heard Abby chuckling behind her.

Abby said, "You never actually get used to it."

Zhang nodded with understanding and said, "And yet, I can't imagine today without her."

Abby's smile turned teary in a flash. "Me either."

"Are you okay, Abby?" Zhang asked as amusement turned to concern.

Her friend wiped a stray tear away quickly and flashed a brave smile. "Yes, I'm sorry. I'm so emotional lately."

"Weddings can do that," Zhang said with sympathy. "Especially weddings that cut your own honeymoon short. Thank you for being here, Abby."

"You might not be thanking me after you've seen me dance," Abby joked, and the mood lightened again.

Zhang thought, *Nothing will ever top seeing my mother joyfully belly dancing in a department store harem outfit.*

Lil burst out of the powder room in her bold-red costume and said, "And now for henna!"

Zhang laughed out loud and hugged Lil.

OK, Mother belly dancing while decorated in henna might require a photograph, because even I'm not going to believe this story tomorrow.

Chapter Sixteen

It was impossible not to compare the somber marriage-contract ceremony with what modern women in Beijing often enjoyed. A wedding wasn't supposed to happen all in one day. These legal documents and the gift exchanges shouldn't be meshed into one event.

Is today even an auspicious date? Since she hadn't been given a choice of day, she hadn't checked the Chinese calendar. *Sometimes it's better not to know.*

Lucky or not, it was her wedding day. There should be fireworks. Pranks. More than one dress for me to change into. Not much was matching how she'd always imagined the day would go. *Except that the result is that I'll be married to the man I love.*

Zhang looked around the rectangular table of what appeared to be a conference room in the palace. Her parents were seated on one side beside her. Across from her sat Rachid and his father.

Both the king and Zhang's father were intently reviewing the contracts that Rachid's attorneys had prepared in both Arabic and Chinese. Her signature would be required at the bottom of the document, but the terms of the dowry and bride price were something that the eldest man in each family had to agree to. Some things were best not challenged, and family honor was one of them, as far as Zhang was concerned. She could have demanded that all of this was her decision to make, but her father was discussing the contract with the king of Najriad and he looked proud to be doing so.

Before either father signed, the king gave her parents a thick red envelope of cash. Rachid then presented her parents with a large gift box of gold coins and jewelry. The king presented Zhang with an equally large gift box of gold jewelry and diamond necklaces. Her mother gave her blankets, a new tea set and more gold.

When all but their signatures were required, King Amir asked Zhang to sit beside Rachid. He stood above them and asked Zhang if she joined into this marriage of her own free will. A week ago that question would have posed a problem, but now Zhang answered yes with sincerity.

The king spoke briefly about how Rachid would honor his wife by caring for her and being her caretaker for all time. He turned to Zhang and gave her the same speech. It was her duty to honor her husband and to be his caretaker for all time. If she agreed, all they had to do was sign the two contracts.

There was no laughter or kissing, just a quick signature and an exchange of rings. Zhang might have been able to handle the rigidity of the ceremony had Rachid smiled at her once. *Was he also thinking of all the things their wedding was not?*

It was not part of a weeklong celebration. The dinner that evening would replace what might otherwise have been a large reception. The next day promised to be a quiet gathering of friends and family.

Maybe that's all you can ask for when you've publicly embarrassed both families on a global level.

Both sets of parents excused themselves after the contracts had been signed. The king bent and kissed Zhang on the head, saying something in Arabic that she didn't understand. Her parents shook Rachid's hand and said they were retiring to their room before dinner.

Alone with her new husband, Zhang was full of equal amounts fear and hope. *Is this where he pulls me to him and kisses me senseless? Possibly deciding to consummate our vows on that sturdy table behind us?*

Maybe he will declare his love for me and tell me that he considered those vows binding. You're mine, Zhang, he'll say in that hot, demanding way of his, and I'll pretend at first that I don't want to be and then I'll let him convince me.

When Rachid stood silently before her, Zhang thought, *Or we'll just stare at each other in a long, painful silence.*

"Dinner is in an hour in the main hall," Rachid said.

And?

Zhang waited.

"Why don't you take the opportunity to rest," he suggested.

Rest?

Luckily we are going to have the rest of our lives together. You'll have plenty of time to make today up to me.

Zhang gave her new husband a small smile. "I am tired. Thank you."

Tired of not knowing what's going on.

Tired of waiting for you to tell me.

"Would you like me to walk you back to your suite?" he asked politely. Zhang wanted to smack him but, deciding that taking advantage of the short time between the signing of the wedding contracts and the celebration dinner was a much better use of her energy, she declined.

Did he have to look so relieved that she turned down his offer?

It would be easy to take Rachid's recent change of mood as evidence that he'd never felt more for her than a passing lust, but Zhang's instincts told her that he was in some sort of trouble. Lust didn't come and go that quickly. There was a reason Rachid was denying the passion between them.

Still, he'd kept his word and ensured that the marriage contracts would protected her assets. So, despite whatever else was going on, he had once again protected her. That meant more to Zhang than the sweet words he'd whispered in the heat of passion.

Not that some passion wouldn't have been nice, but she knew that things like finances, weight and lust fluctuated in even the best marriage. *However, integrity and character did not.*

Rachid is a good man.
My man.

Zhang knocked once on the door of Jeremy's room, opened it and entered without waiting for his permission. He was sitting on the edge of his bed, still bent over and in the act of tying of his shoes. He was dressed in a suit as if he were attending their celebration dinner.

He stood, slid on his other shoe and tied it while hopping toward her. "Zhang? What are you doing here?"

She scanned the room and didn't waste time with niceties. "Did you bring your laptop?"

He pointed to the small desk that was more of a decoration than a workstation. "I'd never leave home without it."

Taking a fortifying breath, Zhang crossed the room to the desk and decided to get straight to the point. "You're not simply here to attend the wedding celebrations."

Jeremy didn't look surprised by her announcement. He said, "I figured."

Zhang touched his closed laptop absently. "What did Dominic tell you?"

Jeremy joined her near the desk. "Nothing, but, come on, people like you don't invite people like me to a major life event unless you need something."

There was no use denying the truth. Zhang held her breath and waited. He stared pointedly at her hand on his laptop until she removed it. Would he help her or not? She couldn't tell.

Meeting her eyes again, he said, "You should know that I don't actually work for Dominic."

"No?" Zhang asked.

Jeremy continued, "It's more of an agreement than an employment situation."

"And your point?"

"If you want my help, it'll cost you." His intelligence wasn't contained to his hacking abilities. He wanted something, and they both knew now that he had the leverage to get it.

"Name your price," Zhang said, shifting her weight to the aggressive stance that was her default.

With a steel-edged tone she was surprised he possessed, he said, "A favor when I ask for one." She'd misjudged this man. Few men could enter the circle of power he'd catapulted himself into, and fewer still could leverage themselves into a position of influence once there. She wouldn't underestimate him again.

"What sort of favor?" Zhang asked, giving him a guarded look.

Leaning a hip against his desk, he folded his arms and said, "Not important. You're asking me to risk my life today. I want your word that you'll go to the same lengths for me if I ask you to."

She needed Jeremy's help to figure out what Rachid was hiding from her, so she didn't have much of a choice. Still, she'd dealt with enough men over her lifetime to know that some boundaries needed to be drawn. "Fine," she said. "Just don't let it be a request that will require me to kill you instead of granting it."

A look of genuine surprise passed over Jeremy's face. Then he smiled at the thought. "Don't worry, Zhang, I have my eyes set on one woman. I always have. If this works out, I'll be one step closer to being the kind of man she wants."

Zhang cocked her head to one side in question.

Jeremy straightened to his full height and clarified, "Dangerous."

"You're doing this for a woman?" she asked incredulously. *My life has truly become a soap opera.*

His mouth set in determination. "Not just any woman. Alethea is everything I've ever wanted. She doesn't think I'm her type, but I'm going to show her that she's wrong."

Trying to inject rational perspective into the situation, Zhang said, "You know you can never tell anyone about any of what happens this weekend."

"No one needs to know. I'll know. Now, what do you want

me to hack?"

Don't second-guess yourself now.

Zhang said, "The palace has an internal server. I need you to access whatever files you can."

Jeremy opened his bag, took out some wires, connected his computer to a port on the wall and turned it on. "What am I looking for?"

Zhang shrugged. "I don't know. Something unusual."

Already opening programs on his screen, Jeremy said, "We're in a palace in Najriad, for cripes sake. Everything is going to look unusual to me."

Fighting the rush of adrenaline that came with nerves, Zhang began to pace behind him. "I have a feeling that the royal family is in danger, but I don't know from whom. There has to be a clue on that server."

Jeremy paused and looked at her over his shoulder. "Is the feeling based on anything concrete?"

"My instincts," Zhang stated firmly.

He continued to study her a moment, then said, "Good enough for me," and turned back to his laptop. "This is interesting," he said.

Zhang spun on her heel and rushed to peer over his shoulder. "What?"

He pointed to a newly translated spreadsheet. "Do you know that they order machine guns as part of the household budget?" He let out a low whistle. "I'd like to go on that shopping run. Two tubs of butter, six M-16s, a box of rounds and some bread, please."

Expelling a frustrated breath, Zhang looked quickly at the door and said, "We don't have much time, Jeremy. Focus."

"Sorry, this is too cool. I don't know how much a Najriadian dinar is worth, but two thousand of them is what it costs to keep all the royal vehicles washed and detailed each month."

"Jeremy!"

"Okay, okay," he muttered. "Hey, wait, here is something."

"What?"

"Last weekend someone ordered five thousand dinars' worth of pillows. That is a classic cover for buying something else. No one needs that many pillows."

Zhang closed her eyes briefly to hide her sudden embarrassment. "That's nothing. Keep looking."

"Hang on, they also claimed to have spent ten thousand dinars on a harem outfit, tapestries and silk scarves and had it all shipped out to the Salnyra Oasis. You can't tell me something kinky wasn't going on there."

No time to reminisce now and not something I want to discuss. "Would you forget about that? Maybe you should check e-mails instead."

Jeremy looked over his shoulder again and asked, "You were at the Oasis last weekend, weren't you?"

"Do you want to live?"

He merely smiled and said, "You are so much cooler than anyone knows."

"Jeremy —"

Thankfully, he turned and began typing again. "Next time, though, you and your prince might want to keep your private purchases off the royal budget spreadsheet—unless you're into that sort of sharing."

Zhang cursed in Mandarin.

Not seeming the least bit bothered, Jeremy laughed. "Listen, this is going to take some time. My software will translate the e-mails, but it's never exact so I'll need a couple of hours to sort through them. Why don't I text you when I find something?"

Zhang checked her watch and reluctantly agreed. Dinner was in less than thirty minutes. "I'll tell everyone that you're not feeling well."

Jeremy said, "Make it convincing or Jeisa will hunt me down and drag me to dinner. It's her personal mission to socialize me." He waved over his shoulder without looking up. "Now, get out of here, I need to concentrate. Especially if we don't have much time."

"Time is the one thing we don't have a lot of."

"Unlike those pillows," he joked.

Zhang gripped the door handle hard enough to instantly whiten her knuckles. Her emotions were running high and she found no humor in his words. Was she really trusting her life and possibly Rachid's to a man who probably considered this mission as challenging as his latest video game?

Do I have a choice?

Sensing that she was still in the room, Jeremy paused and said, "Dominic brought me here because he knows I'm the best. I can stop now if you feel that he's wrong."

There was something unsettling about Jeremy's confidence. Did he know how quickly the situation could turn deadly? "This is dangerous, even if you don't find anything."

Jeremy looked across the room at her. "I don't know about you, Zhang, but I'm tired of settling for what I thought my life had to be. I'd rather die this weekend fighting for my dreams than spend the next fifty years as the man I was. "

Zhang thought about the times when she had felt the same and said, "Be very careful what you wish for, Jeremy. It doesn't always turn out the way we plan." With that, she quickly opened the door and reentered the hallway.

As she stepped away from Jeremy's room, she sensed that she wasn't the only one in the hallway. *Ghalil.* His disapproval was clear, but he didn't confront her. He turned away and strode down the hall in the opposite direction. She could only imagine what he thought she was doing with Jeremy.

Shit.

I need a Plan B.

Chapter Seventeen

Their wedding dinner was a painfully formal affair that, thankfully for Zhang's plans, Ghalil attended. Hopefully he was still figuring out how to take her down and hadn't already sent guards to Jeremy's room. They wouldn't like what they found.

Zhang doubted that the young man's expression would be so dark if he'd already uncovered her secret. No, he wouldn't be able to keep his excitement to himself.

Zhang studied the somber group. The king sat at the head of the table. Hadia was seated at his side, and next to her sat Ghalil and his mother. It was the first time Zhang had seen the woman who had made excuses all week to avoid meeting her. She was appropriately covered and, although she sat tall in her seat, Zhang sensed that she felt uncomfortable being on display. Her eyes remained lowered most of the time.

The king had made a safe choice with his second spouse. Beautiful, reserved, respectfully quiet and Arab. Nothing that would offend. Very likely what his people considered the perfect wife.

My exact opposite.

Zhang snuck a look at her new husband. He was seated next to her, on the other side of his father, and looked every bit of the sheikh he was.

He caught her looking at him and his lips set in a determined line. Beneath the cover of the table, his hand sought hers. She entwined her fingers with his, clinging to hope as she searched his face for some hint that he was still the man who had sworn that they would spend the rest of their lives together.

He bent his head and said so that only she could hear, "No matter what happens, don't get involved. Promise me."

She hedged. "I don't understand."

"Promise me."

Unable to look into those tormented black eyes and lie, she said, "No."

His face set in harsh lines.

The king stood and, as he began to speak, his voice carried easily over the respectfully subdued volume of those at the table. "I would like to thank everyone for sharing in this celebration tonight. Some of you have traveled far to be with us. Some of you had to change your plans due to the unexpectedness of this joyous event. Your kindness will be remembered." He nodded at Rachid and smiled. "If my son can pull his eyes away from his new bride for a moment, I know that he would also like to say a few words."

Rachid released Zhang's hand and stood, bowing to his father before turning to his guests. "I would also like to thank everyone here today. I didn't know when I attended a wedding of an old college friend that I would be inviting him to mine so soon."

Across the table, Dominic nodded in acknowledgement of his reference. Light laughter from several guests followed Rachid's words.

Rachid continued, "Since this is a gathering of many of those who are important to me, I hope you will allow me to take advantage of this opportunity to make an announcement."

His father frowned up at him, obviously not happy to be taken by surprise. Still, he didn't stop his son.

"As you know, I have agreed to accept the royal crown on my next birthday. However, with my father's blessing, I would like to move the coronation up. So, with your permission, Father, I would put forth October first as the date of my coronation and our next large day of celebration."

The room was absolutely quiet as guests and family waited for the king's response. Amir's smile didn't quite reach his eyes as he said, "Nothing would bring me greater pleasure. Of course you have my blessing."

Ghalil stood, his face red with emotion.

His father looked at his youngest and said, "Let your next words be those of congratulations, my son, or let them die unspoken on your lips." When Ghalil said nothing, his father said harshly, "Then sit."

The air hummed with the young man's fury, but he did as his father instructed. His mother put a hand on his arm, but he shook it off and glared at the table.

Rachid spoke as if the exchange between his father and brother hadn't occurred. "Let's eat."

King and prince took their seats simultaneously, a sign that power was already being conceded.

In the silence that followed, Lil's stage whisper to Jake was easily audible to the room. "I feel like we should clap."

Jake shook his head in wonder, but his smile made clear her comment hadn't embarrassed him. He raised his hands and clapped three times slowly. By the third clap, everyone around the table had joined in with enthusiasm.

As the applause gradually faded, the king looked down the table and, with a twinkle of mischief in his eyes, asked, "Dominic, how are you enjoying your stay this weekend?"

Dominic flashed the confident smile he was known for. "Much better than my last visit, Your Excellency."

"Good," the king said. "Perhaps now things will settle down."

Zhang looked across at the prince who was still visibly furious and who unfortunately knew that she'd gone to see Jeremy. He'd use that information against her as soon as he figured out how.

What she couldn't quite understand was why Rachid would move up his acceptance of a title he wasn't sure he wanted. Especially if something foul was afoot.

Unless he thought someone didn't want him to take the crown.

Had there been a threat? Her heart sped up at the thought.

Was that what he was asking her not to get involved in?

The more she thought back to how quickly his mood had changed, the more she felt her guess was right.

Moving up the coronation would force the hand of whoever was trying to stop him.

You'd only do that if you didn't know who posed the threat. Is that what you're doing? Trying to draw your enemy out? Oh, God, Rachid. You are not allowed to get yourself killed when I just realized that I love you.

She reached for contact beneath the table and shuddered when his large hand closed over hers. She wanted to yank on it and demand that he tell her everything, but she doubted he would even if he'd had the privacy to do so.

He smiled down at her and she swore silently, *I'm going to save you, Rachid, if I don't kill you first for not trusting me.*

Chapter Eighteen

Zhang was both relieved and concerned when, at the end of the meal, Rachid informed her that he had some business to address before he could come to her that evening. Another woman might have been hurt to be dismissed by her groom on their wedding night, but another woman wouldn't have spent half the meal hoping he would accept her request for some time alone to rest.

And by "rest," I mean "find out if Jeremy has uncovered anything yet." Going directly back to his room was too risky, since there was a good chance Ghalil would be waiting for her to do just that. Instead, Zhang headed to the suite of the only person crazy enough to help her.

Alone and still dressed in the suit he'd worn to dinner, Dominic answered the door. With a quick glance over her shoulder to make sure no one was watching, Zhang slipped inside.

"I need to talk to you, Dominic," she said.

"Isn't this a conversation you should have with your mother?" he asked dryly.

Already short of temper, Zhang asked, "What the hell are you talking about?"

Dominic closed the door and motioned for Zhang to sit. Suddenly serious, he said, "Sorry, an attempt at wedding humor. What do you need?"

Zhang paced the small area between the couches. "Jeremy is set up and searching files now. I told him I'd return after dinner, but Gahlil saw me leave his room. I don't know what he thought I was doing there but it's too dangerous for me to return. Can you do it? I don't trust using our cell phones here.

Something's not right."

Dominic crossed the room to where Zhang stood and agreed. "As usual, your instincts are right. Rachid's announcement felt strategic—like he was trying to goad someone into action. Do you think it's his brother?"

"I don't know, but I'm hoping Jeremy found something. Will you help me?"

Abby stepped out of the bedroom, covered in a long blue silk nightgown and robe. "Help you do what?"

Zhang and Dominic looked at each other guiltily, like two children caught red-handed and trying to come up with a convincing lie.

Abby crossed the room, stopping just in front of her husband. Hands placed angrily on her hips, Abby said, "Dom, you promised me that we wouldn't keep secrets from each other."

Dominic took her hands in his and said, "I don't want you involved in this, Abby. It's too dangerous."

With her chin held at a stubborn slant, Abby said, "Even more of a reason why I should know what is going on."

Just as stubborn, Dominic shook his head and said, "No, Abby. The less you know the better."

"You can't do this, Dom," Abby pleaded.

Looking unhappy, but set in his decision, Dominic said, "Zhang needs my help. Give me thirty minutes —"

"I'm pregnant," Abby blurted out, sudden tears filling her eyes.

Dom sat down on the couch behind him with a heavy thud. "Pregnant?"

Abby sat beside her now pasty-white husband, took one of his hands and laid it on her stomach. "Yes. Do you understand why you have to stop seeing yourself as indestructible?"

When Dominic spoke, his voice shook with emotion. "I'm going to be a father."

Abby nodded, tears flowing down her cheeks. "Yes. And that means that you have to stop risking your life like it doesn't matter, because it does. It matters to me. And it matters to our baby." She turned to look up at Zhang and pleaded, "Please, don't ask him to do something dangerous. I know you've been very kind to me, but I can't lose him now."

Dominic pulled his wife to his side, wiped her tears away with one hand and looked down into her pleading eyes. He said, "I'll be fine, Abby."

When he looked up, his eyes were full of such sadness that a profound sense of shame settled over Zhang. It was easy to forget that Dominic wasn't a bulletproof hero, just a man who loved his wife and was torn between helping a friend and protecting his new family. She couldn't ask him to risk more than he had.

The outer door of the suite flew open and Lil burst in. As soon as she saw Abby crying, she rushed to her side and said, "What happened? Tell me it wasn't something I did."

Abby straightened from Dom and sniffed. "No, this time I'm the awful person."

No, I'm the one being selfish. This is my problem. Zhang said, "No, you're not, Abby. You're doing what any good mother would do—you're fighting for your family."

Lil said, "I don't understand."

Laughing and crying at the same time, Abby said, "I'm pregnant."

"Oh, my God, I'm so happy for you." Joining her sister on the couch, Lil wrapped an arm around her and said, "Okay, so why is everyone so miserable? You all look like I felt when —" She stopped abruptly and stood. "Hang on, I'm seeing a pattern here. Why did we bring Jeremy? Didn't you learn anything from what I did?" She looked around at the stunned expressions of the three she'd walked in on and said, "You might as well tell me everything or I'll only try to find out on my own, and you all know how that works out."

Zhang said, "I shouldn't have involved any of you. I'm sorry."

Abby said, "No, Zhang. I was wrong. Dominic's right. I

can't let my fear stop us from helping the people we love."

Shaking her head, Zhang said, "No, you were right. This is my problem."

Dominic stood. "It's too dangerous for you to go back there, Zhang."

Jake walked through the open door. "Go where?"

Dominic's explanation held everyone's attention long enough to allow Zhang to back out of the room unnoticed.

One hand casually pocketed, Rachid stood beneath the dim lighting of the covered patio that overlooked the inner courtyard of the palace. Realistically, he knew that his plan to draw the traitor out might take weeks, if it worked at all. He was counting on his enemy being tempted by the chaos of the wedding weekend. Temptation was another reason he'd avoided being alone with Zhang. He couldn't involve her in this.

He'd expected Zhang to be hurt by his withdrawal, but she'd looked almost relieved when he'd said he needed some time to himself before their wedding night. He shouldn't care, but the indifference with which she accepted the news had stung. Yes, he'd already decided to honor her request and keep their relationship platonic, but a part of him had hoped it would be as difficult for her as it was for him.

He froze at the unmistakable sound of metal sliding against metal as a round was racked in a gun chamber just behind his head. Moving himself away from the watchful eyes of the guardsmen had apparently worked. Without turning, Rachid said in Arabic, "You didn't waste any time."

He waited, praying that the voice didn't belong to someone close to him.

The male voice that answered wasn't one he recognized. It said, "It didn't have to come to this. You should have left when you had a chance."

Rachid stood tall. "I came home because my father asked me to, and I stayed for the same reason. Will you shoot me in the back of the head like a coward?" When the man didn't answer, Rachid turned and recognized the traitor as one of the royal security guards. "You know you'll never get away with killing me."

The man kept his firearm pointed directly in Rachid's face. He said, "The gun will be traced back to your American friends. No one will suspect one of the guardsmen."

"Are you willing to bet your life on that?"

The man shrugged. "Too late to worry about it now, isn't it? You can't live since you know who I am."

Deciding to stall until either an opportunity to fight presented itself or help arrived, Rachid said calmly, "You pledged your life to protect the royal family. Why do this?"

The man's face contorted with anger. "You're not one of us. You and your foreign wife will make a mockery of the crown. I *am* protecting the royal family," he said with conviction. "I'm protecting it from you."

Out of the corner of his eye, Rachid saw movement in the doorway behind the gunman. Relief quickly turned to real fear when he saw who had joined them.

A few moments earlier, Zhang had decided that texting Jeremy was not going to be enough. She headed back to his room and, as she expected, found Ghalil lingering in the hallway.

Fight, Hadia had said. *Fight for Rachid and the rest will take care of itself.* Zhang came to a fast decision. She walked directly up to Ghalil and asked, "Are you looking for me?"

Ghalil sneered down at her. "I was waiting to see if you had the gall to return to your boyfriend's room on your own wedding night."

Zhang stepped closer, invading his space and thundering up at him. "Are you so blinded by your jealousy of your brother that you honestly can't see what's going on?"

Ghalil grabbed her by the arm and snarled, "I'm not jealous

of my brother."

Zhang said, "Pride is the worst shield because it leaves you both vulnerable and wrong at the same time."

The young man's eyes blazed with fury. "Wrong is seeking out another man when you're married to my brother."

"Suddenly you care about Rachid?"

"I've always cared about him." *Good. Maybe there is hope for you after all.*

"Then prove it. Put your pettiness aside and help him before he gets himself killed."

The young man's hand tightened on Zhang's arm. "What are you talking about?"

"Didn't you think Rachid's dinner announcement was oddly timed?"

"Not if he's eager for the crown."

"But he isn't, Ghalil. Even you know that. So why move the date up?"

Ghalil countered, "Because he fears the embarrassment you'll bring our house?"

Zhang ripped her arm out of his grip and gave his chest a shove. "Listen, you little yipping puppy, I love your brother, and if you're any indication of the support he has here, he's going to need all the help I can give him. He made that announcement to draw someone out. I know it. There is a traitor in the palace."

Ghalil shook his head in confusion. "I would know if that were the case. Rachid would have taken his concerns to the royal security if he had any, or told me."

"Unless he didn't know who to trust."

"If all of this is true, what are you doing with this American man?"

Zhang sighed. She didn't want to expose her actions, but she needed his help. "Do you believe me?"

The young man wavered. "Some of what you say makes sense."

"Then help me." She looked up into her brother-in-law's

face and deepened her plea. "Help me save your brother."

Ghalil nodded, suddenly looking years older as he straightened his shoulders and stepped up to the responsibility she'd laid at his feet. "Okay."

Looking quickly down the hallway in both directions, Zhang pulled Ghalil into Jeremy's room. Jeremy peered up from his laptop and said, "If you're looking for someone to knock him out, my boxing lessons start next week."

Zhang said, "He's here to help us."

Jeremy asked sarcastically, "Is that wise?"

Zhang dragged Ghalil over to where Jeremy was seated. "Did you find anything?"

Jeremy shook his head. "Nothing worth texting you about."

Ghalil broke away from Zhang and looked over Jeremy's shoulder. His face went red with rage. "That's the palace server." He scanned the document Jeremy was reading. "You've translated our e-mails."

Zhang said, "We had to, Ghalil. There may be something in them that will reveal who the traitor is."

"From where I'm standing, it looks like you, Zhang. You'll rot in jail for this betrayal."

Jeremy stood and moved to block the door. His mouth twisted with irony. "I haven't hit anyone since middle school, but maybe it comes back like riding a bike." He cracked his knuckles. He stood a good head above the young prince.

Zhang quickly moved between the two men. "You won't have to touch him, Jeremy, because he's going to wake up and realize that we are the good guys here."

Ghalil asked harshly, "How do I know that?"

Zhang said, "Would I have involved you if we weren't? Why would I show you what we were doing?"

Ghalil first studied the tall man who blocked his path and then Zhang who, as she waited, was poised to tackle him if he tried to leave. "You really think you can find the traitor online?"

Zhang let out a shaky breath. "Yes, if he's not working alone. The problem is that we don't know what to look for. If you read over the e-mails, maybe you could find something."

A heavy silence dragged on. Finally Ghalil said, "Show me."

Jeremy led the way back to the small work area and motioned toward the chair. "I have them all listed here. Dig in."

With one last look at Zhang and Jeremy, Ghalil sat down in front of the laptop and started reading. He leaned forward as he became more absorbed in the process.

Jeremy whispered, "You shouldn't have involved him, Zhang."

Zhang muttered, "I didn't have a choice."

Jeremy said, "He's just a kid."

Zhang looked at the young prince and said, "He's twenty. If people stop treating him like a child, he'll stop acting like one."

Ghalil said something in Arabic, then switched to English. "It looks like you're right. One of the guards, Kalim, has been communicating with the general of the National Guard. It sounds like the border raids were coordinated. This is not good. They've been watching Rachid and looking for ways to discredit him. I'm sure they took the photo of you and Rachid on Dominic's island. It looks like Kalim has been keeping the general apprised of my father's whereabouts. Here, he even details how to attack my father's dummy motorcade. Why would he boldly write about this in e-mails?"

Jeremy said, "Those messages were encrypted and sent as hidden attachments. Most people wouldn't know to look for them."

In shock, Ghalil shook his head. "A member of the Royal Guardsmen and he's not working alone. Are they trying to wage a coup? Why just target Rachid?"

Zhang said, "Who knows? But we have to tell him."

Ghalil stood and said, "I'll do it."

Zhang corrected, "We'll do it."

Jeremy jumped in and said, "I'm going, too. It's always better to be a hero than one of the expendable extras."

Zhang said, "This isn't a movie, Jeremy. Stay here."

Jeremy took out a small device and said, "You need me." When neither she nor Ghalil agreed, he added, "Is anyone else tracking Rachid via his cell phone? I didn't think so. Come on."

Chapter Nineteen

When Rachid saw Zhang in the doorway behind the gunman, his breath caught in his throat. Couldn't that woman listen to him just this once? Royal Guardsmen were the most highly trained soldiers in the royal military. There was a good chance that Zhang was going to witness her new husband die, something he would have given anything to spare her from. He briefly hoped that she'd see the gun and be smart enough to run, but when their eyes met across the patio he saw the truth in her eyes.

It would take more than a gun for her to leave him.

His heart twisted in his chest.

Ghalil appeared immediately behind her. Confusion swirled within Rachid. He refused to believe that his brother was involved in this, but why would he bring Zhang?

Unless he needs both of us dead.

His younger brother wasn't as restrained as his wife had been. He said, "Rachid!" as soon as he saw him.

Hearing the younger prince's voice, the guard turned his head for just a moment. Rachid tried to knock the gun out of his would-be assassin's hand but failed. The guard's fist connected with Rachid's jaw and sent him flying back.

Ghalil rushed forward, but the guard turned and pointed the gun at his chest.

Rachid was on his feet in a heartbeat and approached the guard from the side. There wasn't time to be relieved that his brother wasn't involved. He addressed the guard. "I'm the one you want. You can justify killing me to yourself, but his blood will stain your very soul and you know it."

Ghalil said, "Put your weapon down, Kalim."

181

The guard said, "Your Highness, you've said yourself that if your brother takes the crown it will be the end of Najriad. The title should be yours."

Ghalil inched closer. His face was tight with guilt. "I did say that, but this isn't what I wanted." He looked across to Rachid and said, "I never meant for this to happen."

I know, little brother. "Ghalil, back away. It's me he wants."

Ghalil didn't. He stood his ground and said, "But it is us that he will have to beat."

The guard rotated the gun back and forth between the two brothers as Rachid continued his slow creep forward.

I can't let you die for me, Ghalil.

Rachid stepped closer, drawing the attention of the gunman, and said, "No one has to die here today."

The guard focused the gun at Rachid's chest and said, "You're wrong. Even if I die, it won't be in vain because you'll come with me. I do this for you, for Prince Ghalil and for Najariad."

Rachid held his breath.

Ghalil jumped forward and reached for the gun. The gunman turned toward the young prince, giving Rachid the chance to grab for the weapon. In the scuffle that ensued, the gun fired and Ghalil fell to the stone patio floor.

Rachid let out a roar of rage and landed a punch that sent the guard flying in one direction and the gun in another. He grabbed the man by the collar of his robe, lifted him off the floor and sent him reeling back with another punch.

A bullet is too good for you. I'm going to kill you with my bare hands.

Before he could reach him again, Rachid saw Jeremy standing over the man, gun in hand. He said, "I've got him, Rachid. Go to your brother."

Ghalil.

Rachid rushed to his brother's side and dropped to his knees. Ghalil was trying to sit up.

"Don't move," Rachid said in Arabic. "You've been shot."

Ghalil grabbed at his brother's hand even as his face began to lose color. He said, "This is my fault. I'm so sorry, Rachid."

Ghalil lost consciousness and Rachid hugged his brother's limp body to him. "Don't die, little brother. Don't you dare die."

In a heartbeat, the courtyard and patio was filled with Royal Guardsmen. The gunman was quickly removed. An emergency medical team appeared so swiftly it was as if they had been called before the shooting. Rachid reluctantly released his brother so they could treat him.

It was only after Ghalil was lifted and strapped to a gurney that Rachid realized Zhang was by his side. He wrapped an arm around her and held her tight. Her eyes filled with tears. She pulled his head down and for a moment he lost himself in her kiss. He wanted to kiss her until she swore to listen to him in the future, or until the fear he'd felt when he thought he could lose her loosened its grip on his chest. As their kiss deepened he forgot everything except how much he loved this woman. Reality came crashing back in and he put her back from him.

The torment in her eyes tore at him, and he swore that he would never be the reason she felt like that again. He would keep her safe, even if that meant losing her.

"I have to go." He motioned to his brother being rolled away. "I may not be back tonight."

Zhang wiped the tears and said, "I'll wait up."

He touched her damp cheek tenderly. "No, sleep in the women's quarters tonight. I'll come for you tomorrow."

She smiled vaguely but didn't argue with him.

Had he finally issued an order she'd follow?

The thought amused him as he rushed off to join his brother in the ambulance. How ironic if she finally became obedient just before he asked her to leave.

Zhang was visibly shaking when her American friends pushed past the guards. Dominic was the first to reach her side. Jake was fast on his heels. A detail of their own security surrounded them, buffering Zhang and clashing somewhat with the royal guards. Weapons were drawn on both sides.

When a man's voice boomed from one of the open patio doors, all of the Royal Guardsmen pointed their rifles down and stood at attention. The man who approached was familiar to Zhang. He was the same guard who had rescued her from her first altercation with Ghalil.

He bowed his head to her and said, "Your Highness, are you hurt?"

"No," Zhang said in a shaky voice.

"Do you require assistance?"

Zhang fought the tears that were a by-product of fading adrenaline and said, "No, these men are my friends."

The head of the Royal Guardsmen issued an order, and his men fell back to positions around the patio. As the guards withdrew, one man remained that caught Dominic's attention. He tensed and motioned to his security to secure the one he didn't recognize.

Zhang quickly interceded and said, "He's with me."

Jeremy stepped into the circle of Dominic's security. "The palace guards have the gunman. I don't think we'll ever see him again. They were speaking Arabic, but I'm pretty sure they were telling him that he wasn't going to live long."

Dominic said, "You should have waited for us, Zhang."

Jeremy intervened. "Rachid would be dead if she had. We cut it close as it was."

The reality of how close she'd come to losing Rachid swept over her, and emotion clogged her throat as tears spilled freely down her face.

Dominic turned on Jeremy. "Now look what you did."

Jeremy went toe-to-toe with Dominic. "Those are tears of gratitude because I saved her prince."

Dominic was about to say something more, but Zhang

stopped him with a light touch to his forearm and said, "He did save Rachid. Without him, I would be crying for an entirely different reason tonight." She tried but couldn't stop the tears from flowing. "When we walked onto the patio and I saw that man holding a gun to Rachid's head, I thought we were too late. Everything I spent the last week worrying about didn't matter. I couldn't lose Rachid so soon after realizing I love him. But I didn't see a way to save him."

Jeremy spoke under his breath to Dominic. "You should probably hug her or something."

Dominic shifted uneasily and said, "I'm not really good with crying women. You do it."

Jeremy protested, "You've known her longer."

Jake stepped forward, pulled Zhang into a warm embrace that she didn't bother to pretend she didn't need, and let her sob into his dress shirt. She wept out the emotions of the week. She cried for the fears she was ready to put aside, the man she'd almost lost and the brother who had finally defended Rachid. When she had settled enough to take a calming breath, she heard Jake say, "Women and children are messy, but you get used to it."

Zhang stepped away from him, dried her eyes and smiled up at the three large men who loomed above her. She didn't have brothers, but she had the next best thing. She straightened her gown and said, "I won't tell anyone that you're all idiots if you don't share how I just lost it."

Dominic said, "Agreed, the less Abby knows about the gunman, the better."

Jake said, "Why don't we walk you back to your suite? I can send Lil over."

Zhang accepted the escort but said, "Tell Lil I'll see her tomorrow."

Jake nodded.

Zhang walked down the hallway with her three tuxedoed bodyguards and their trailing security guards. Normally she'd love to see Lil, but she had no intention of waiting patiently for

Rachid to come see her tomorrow.

I don't want to be alone.

And I'm not going to be—not if I have anything to do with it.

Chapter Twenty

A little past three in morning, Rachid wearily entered his private suite at the palace. When he'd left the hospital, Ghalil was stable and, although he'd lost a lot of blood, the doctors had said that none of his major organs had been damaged. He'd make a full recovery.

Rachid wasn't sure the same could be said for him. He shed his clothing as if removing it would somehow lesson some of the weight of his thoughts. For now, the story was contained and the official statement regarding Prince Ghalil's hospital visit was exhaustion. *I'm sure being shot is exhausting.* The treating staff had all been spoken to and asked to sign nondisclosures. Luckily, no foreign press had been present at the hospital. *Najriadian National News* would print whatever the royal family instructed it to say. King Amir had poured a heavy amount of the country's oil fortune into improving the living conditions of his people, but the same hand that reached out with kindness could just as quickly strike a deadly blow when opposed.

An effective monarch needed to be both loved and feared.

I'm neither.

Nude and bone tired, Rachid stepped beneath the hot sting of his shower. He absently washed as his mind raced. He should be celebrating the roundup of his enemies. Thanks to Dominic's hacker, Marshid had been able to surprise all of those involved. Even the general implicated in the emails had been caught unaware thanks to the swiftness of the response from the most trusted royal guardsmen. Punishments would be harsh, fast and outside of the public view.

Rachid knew he should be figuring out how to explain the

actions of his friends to his father. Or, at the very least, begin to formulate a plan so that none of this would ever happen again.

Instead, his mind kept returning to what was now the worst moment of his life: that brief time when he thought he would be the reason Zhang died. When he'd seen her in the doorway of the patio, nothing beyond saving her had mattered. His life, sadly even the life of his brother, had come second in his need to protect her.

Rachid turned off the water, toweled dry and padded to his bedroom while wrapping the plush material around his waist.

In another time or life, he would have proclaimed his love for Zhang, but how could he ask her to give up her freedom and career when he wasn't sure he could keep her safe? He closed his eyes and shook his head at the thought of Zhang hacking into the royal server and taking on his security like some secret agent. All that disobedience had saved his life, and he owed her the same selflessness.

No matter how it looked to his people or what his father said, he would let Zhang go tomorrow. If she needed the cover of his name, they could stay married for whatever amount of time she requested. But he wouldn't keep her in Najriad. She deserved the freedom she'd fought so hard for. And she would have it.

The light on one side of the room flipped on. There, in the middle of his bed, was the very woman who was tormenting his thoughts. Dressed in a red satin slip of a nightgown, she pushed back the bed sheets and stood, facing him boldly as if they'd always shared a room together.

"How is your brother?" she asked.

Rachid didn't move. The sight of her, mussed from sleep and reaching for him, was almost too tempting to resist. She deserved better than this, better than him. He turned away before he gave in to the overwhelming desire to lose himself in her arms. "He'll recover." With his back to her, Rachid said, "You need to leave, Zhang. You shouldn't be here. I told you that we'd talk tomorrow."

Instead of doing as he said, she moved to stand behind him and laid one of her delicate hands on his back. He shuddered with need for her but didn't turn.

"What's wrong, Rachid? Why turn me away?"

He clung to the last of his resolve and insisted, "I was wrong to push you to marry me. You can go home with your friends tomorrow."

"And if I don't want to?"

"You have to."

As she slipped around to stand in front of him, he clenched his hands at his sides to stop from pulling her into his chest. He was trying to do the right thing, but the wrong thing was quickly starting to feel like a better option. He fought his weakness.

"Why?" she whispered, and he made the mistake of looking down into those beautiful dark eyes of hers.

Raggedly, he confessed, "I love you."

Her head flew back, exposing her long, lovely neck while she laughed softly. She said, "I wouldn't consider that a deal breaker for a marriage. Some might even say it's a good thing."

Giving in to his overwhelming need to touch her, he pulled her against him and simply hugged her. Desire shook him again and he said, "Just before Ghalil was shot, I saw you in the doorway, and suddenly it didn't matter that I had a gun to my head. I have never been so afraid in my life. Nothing mattered except your safety, and I wasn't sure I could save you. You can't stay here, Zhang. You have to see that."

Zhang wrapped her arms around his waist and laid her head on his chest. "No, I don't see that at all."

He groaned and pulled her closer. "I'm no Prince Charming, Zhang. I'm just a man—a man with a crushing amount of responsibility. I wish I could tell you that things will be better next week or next year, but I have to face that they may never be better. Violence may always be part of my life and I can't ask you to accept that. I won't put you at risk again."

Raising her head so she could look up into his face, Zhang said, "You don't get to make that decision. You don't get to tell me what I can or can't handle. It's a violent world out there, Rachid. The small village I grew up in held its own dangers. I wouldn't have armed men on my payroll if my own life were without risk. Danger is part of life. No one is immune from it, no matter how they may try to insulate themselves. No, I don't have a problem with danger."

When Rachid would have said something, Zhang pinched the skin on his ribs and continued on angrily. "What I struggle with is that you think you have to shoulder all of the responsibility yourself. You say you love me, but what exactly is it that you love? Because I'm not sure you see me. I fought for everything I have and I'm willing to help you fight for Najriad, but I need to know that you love me the way I am. It's your lack of faith in my ability to share the weight of this that makes me angry. And I suspect that your brother feels the same."

"Ghalil is just a boy."

"No, he's a man who took a bullet for you and is just as willing to give his life for his family and country as you are. Maybe it's time the two of you sat down and talked about that. You're not alone."

Thinking back over the conversations he'd had with his brother, Rachid realized that he'd cultivated the issues he had with Ghalil. By treating his younger brother like a child, he had pushed him to prove his manhood. Of course Ghalil would feel threatened and insulted. *How didn't I see that?* Rachid ran his hand through the shoulder-length hair of the most beautiful woman he'd ever seen. "Princess Zhang, how did you get so wise?"

Zhang laughed with self-deprecation. "Trust me, I'm no Cinderella, Rachid. I'm just a woman—a woman with very strong opinions and a problem accepting authority. I can't promise you that life with me will be easy, but when we're together I feel like I'm —"

He finished the sentence for her. "Home."

Tears filled her eyes. "Yes. Home. And it doesn't matter to

me if we live in Najriad or on the moon as long as I'm with you. Choose us, Rachid, and we'll work everything else out."

The last wall in Rachid's heart crumbled and he stepped back to lift her nightgown over her head. He kissed her until they were shaking against each other from a mixture of the intensity of their emotions and a desire to express their love in hot actions. "How did I find such an incredible wife?"

Standing exposed and proud before the worshiping eyes of her husband, Zhang joked, "I have this thing for sheikhs."

Rachid lifted her easily in his arms and tossed her onto the bed behind her. "Sheikhs in general, or one in particular?" He dropped his towel and crawled across the large bed to loom over her.

She laughed up at him, "I'm not sure. There was one who used to do this thing with his tongue that I loved. Was that you?"

With a growl, Rachid pounced. He spread her legs and positioned himself between her knees. Ever so slowly he began to kiss the sensitive flesh of her thighs. His large hands lifted her rump and held her so he could savor the path to her. His hot tongue warmed and teased her stomach and finally parted her folds and delved in with expertise.

Zhang threw her head back, grabbed the bedding beside her and exclaimed passionately, "Yes, that's what I remember."

Rachid laughed against her and said, "Are you sure? Because I could spend the night reminding you." He circled and lapped at her most sensitive spot while his hands firmly massaged her ass. "My own memory is fuzzy, but I seem to remember that you like this..." He slid a finger within her and rolled it gently, enjoying how Zhang clenched around him.

He repositioned himself so he could continue to stroke her intimately while he looked down into her flushed face. "God, I hope you meant what you said, because I don't have the strength to let you go."

Zhang circled his face with both of her hands and pulled him down for a kiss. She said, "I love you, Rachid. I'm not going anywhere." When her lips met his, coherent conversation was replaced by an urgency on both sides that would no longer be denied. The rest of the night was filled with intense pleasure, hot whispered suggestions and shared satisfaction until they fell asleep, exhausted and spent in each other's arms.

Half-reclining, half-sitting against Rachid the next morning, Zhang sampled the breakfast breads that the house staff had delivered to their room. She popped a small bite into his mouth and shivered in response to the feel of his lips closing around her fingers.

Rachid ran his hand possessively down her bare back and gave her rump a light smack. "We haven't talked about you using a hacker to access the royal server."

Zhang smiled and rubbed his chest with one hand. "Genius, wasn't it?"

Rachid caught her hand and held it to him. "Or treason. What if it hadn't worked out the way it did? You're lucky you didn't land yourself in prison."

Dismissing what had clearly not happened, Zhang said, "Now that would be a fun fantasy, but I'd rather be the jailor. You could be the very naughty international spy whom I have to interrogate."

Amusement rumbled through Rachid's chest and he said, "You and your fantasies! That's how this all started."

Zhang didn't want to think about how one decision had changed her whole life, because then she would have to consider how close she and Rachid had come to never being together. She remembered her American friends cautioning her at Abby's bachelorette party to choose her wedding escort with care and chuckled at how right they had been. One seemingly random event had changed everything. She shook off the past and refocused on the delectable present. "Exactly. Are you telling me that you wouldn't love to be tied up while I torture you slowly?" She ran a hand lightly down his flat stomach and muscular thigh, avoiding touching what was eagerly springing to life and begging for her touch. "Again and again until you beg for release?"

He pulled her beneath him and pinned both hands above her head. "What if I like being in control?"

She rubbed her bare chest against his, loving how his breathing quickened and how he burned for her. She whispered against his lips. "We could take turns."

He smiled and murmured, "I like the way you think."

Chapter Twenty-One

Still joined together, Rachid and Zhang jumped at the knock on the outer door of his suite. Zhang dismissed it, settled back into position and asked, "Did you order more food?"

Rachid shook his head and eased out from under his wife. "Stay here, I'll check who it is."

She rolled onto her back, pulled the sheet up over her chest and closed her eyes again. "See, I can follow orders."

He leaned down, kissed her relaxed lips and suggested playfully, "Only because you're feeling too lazy to get up."

Eyes closed, Zhang returned the kiss, then stretched and smiled into a pillow. "If you wanted feisty this morning you shouldn't have tired me out last night."

Not moving from his position above her, Rachid teased, "Is that all it takes to get an obedient wife? Wild marathon sex sprees? You should have said something earlier."

Zhang's eyes flew open and she swatted at him with a pillow. He easily avoided the hit.

The knock on the door was louder the second time.

Rachid picked up the white sirwal pants he'd worn the night before and padded to the door. His stomach flipped when he saw it was Marshid, the head of the Royal Guardsmen. "Is it Ghalil?" he asked in a rush.

"No, Your Highness. The latest report from the hospital is that your brother is awake and out of danger. However, the king wishes to see you and your wife in the library."

Rachid looked quickly back at the bedroom door he'd closed behind him. "Did he say why?"

"No, Your Highness."

Rachid nodded and said, "Tell him that we will meet him

in fifteen minutes."

With a slight bow the guard left, and Rachid returned to the bedroom. He said, "My father wants to see both of us."

Zhang sat straight up in bed. "Is he angry?"

Rachid shrugged, but sat on the edge of the bed. "I would never let anyone hurt you."

Zhang leaned forward and touched the very serious man she'd made up her mind to spend the rest of her life with. "I know you wouldn't."

"He may question the advisability of me taking the title in October."

"Do you want it?" she asked and watched his expression tighten.

"Yes and no. What if I'm not the right man? What if my brother is correct and I'm not Arab enough?"

Zhang scooted closer until she was kneeling in front of her husband, and then she took both of his hands in hers. "I wasted too much of my life trying to decide who I am, and I didn't figure it out until I met you. I'm not a traditional, family-oriented woman from a small village in China. I'm not a die-hard, successful career woman of the world. I am a wonderfully complex combination of both those people. My culture is the beautiful canvas on which I have painted the details of my life. Who would I be without either of those elements?" Rachid took her hand tightly in his and absorbed her words. "I don't think you will succeed here until you stop denying that the same is true for you. It seems like since you've come home to Najriad, you've tried to deny the man you were for the past two decades. Half a man cannot lead a country. But what if your experience out there gives you the strength you need to rule here? You think you can only be a good king if the people love and fear you, but those ways are outdated. If you stay and show your people what you can do for them—really show them—they will love and respect you. Maybe that's why your father sent you away—so you would be a bridge between the past and the future."

Expelling a harsh breath, Rachid pulled Zhang into his arms and held her tightly against his wildly beating heart. "When I'm with you I feel invincible."

Zhang hugged him back. "I feel the same way."

Rachid smiled into her hair and said, "Invincible or not, we shouldn't make my father wait."

They rushed through a shared shower and quickly threw on clothing. To Zhang's surprise, Rachid chose a charcoal suit instead of his traditional white thobe. He added the white headdress with black accent rope. The combination was impressive and powerful. The doubt she'd sensed earlier was gone from the proud man who stood tall before her.

He held out his hand to Zhang said, "Come, it's time for my father to meet his son."

King Amir didn't look pleased to see either of them when they joined him in the library. He left the view from the large window to take a seat, then waved at the two chairs near him and motioned for Rachid and Zhang to join him. They did.

And waited.

The silence was painful and prolonged.

Zhang was the first to speak. "Your Highness, I'm so sorry about Ghalil. I would have never involved him if I had known that the danger was imminent."

Rachid leaned forward, placed a hand on Zhang's arm and said, "The fault is mine, Father. I should have told you of my plan."

Raising one impatient hand, the king said, "Enough. It's time for both of you to listen."

They sat back in their chairs.

Nothing about the king's stern expression implied that they would like what he was going to say. "I have spent half the night sorting through yesterday's events with everyone from my advisor to each of the remaining guardsmen. Zhang, you accessed the royal server without permission. You brought

196

strangers into my home and spent time alone with the men in their private quarters. This isn't behavior befitting a future queen. You must learn to respect our ways."

I would do it all again, Zhang thought, but for Rachid's sake, she put her pride aside and said, "I will. I do."

The king continued harshly, "Rachid, do you believe that you will be able to control your wife in the future?"

Rachid looked at Zhang and then boldly met his father's eyes. "No, and I don't want to." His father frowned, and Zhang worried for just a moment until her husband added, "I love her the way she is. If you don't feel that she is fit to be queen then I am not fit to be king, because she is part of me." He took her hand in his. "Wherever she goes, I will go."

His father's voice boomed through the small room. "You would abdicate your crown and walk away?"

Rachid squared his shoulders and squeezed Zhang's hand in his. "Not unless you want me to. You once asked me to go into the world and bring back the best of what I found." He held up Zhang's hand and kissed it. "That's exactly what I did. Proximus could give our people a new source of revenue, and my fierce wife has the expertise to help make my dream a reality. Together, we will fight for causes we feel strongly about—here and across the globe. Najriad is my country, but Zhang is my home."

"I see," the king said and rubbed his short beard thoughtfully. "I'm not happy with the way you and your bride dealt with this breach of security." Zhang and Rachid held their breath. The king said, "However, I am indebted to your wife."

Zhang wasn't sure which of her actions of the past week could have earned his gratitude, since she still blamed herself for Ghalil's injury.

The king said, "Daughter, because of you, my sons have proven to themselves and to the world that they would die for each other. I have always known that for Najriad to survive they would have to stand together." He looked into his son's eyes and said, "I know the price you paid honoring my request to leave, Rachid, but I didn't see another way. My father ruled with fear and I grew up with a tolerance for bloodshed. You needed to experience more than I had. I have done many things that I regret, but I don't regret you. You will make a fine king, and your brother will help you navigate these difficult times. Together, you can bring a real peace to our people."

Rachid said, "Father, I will dedicate my life to improving and protecting our people."

The king nodded with approval and said, "That's all I could ask for." A gleam entered his eye as he returned his attention to his daughter-in-law. "That, and grandchildren. At least four."

Zhang jolted in her seat and looked at Rachid. "Four?" she asked in shock.

Rachid smiled. "You want more?"

"Only if you grow a uterus," Zhang tossed back.

Both Rachid and his father threw back their heads and laughed.

A bit of sadness entered the king's eyes as he studied his new daughter-in-law. He said, "Rachid, your mother was outspoken also. I spent our time together trying to change her. In the end, she changed me."

Zhang's eyes filled with tears.

The king stood and smiled down at the next generation. "I still miss her." He touched Zhang's cheek softly and said, "You chose well, Son."

Rachid stood and pulled his wife up beside him. "I'd like to take the credit, but rumor has it that she chose me."

The king looked interested in the story, but Rachid didn't offer more details. *Thank God,* Zhang thought. Some stories needed to be cleaned up a bit before they joined a family's history.

Mommy, tell us again how you picked Daddy from a digital lineup of the world's most eligible bachelors.

Did you really sleep with him the first night you met?

What does it mean that his proposal was orgasmic?

There wasn't a single moment Zhang would change about their journey since it had taken all of it to bring them together, but certain aspects could be paraphrased for the retelling.

Love at first sight.

Discovering themselves and each other in the face of adversity.

Maybe even that Grandma Hadia taught Grandma Xiaoli how to belly dance.

Chapter Twenty-Two

A month later, Zhang stood wrapped in Rachid's embrace on the balcony of his palace suite as they watched the sun set behind the city's skyline. Rachid nuzzled his wife's neck.

"I heard from Abby," Zhang said. "They're finally back from their honeymoon."

Rachid said, "I spoke to Dominic. After everything that happened here, I was relieved to hear that his server went online without a hitch."

"Do you think they'll come back for your coronation, or did our wedding weekend scare them off?" Zhang asked into the night sky.

"Dominic is a bit of a nervous wreck regarding his wife's health lately, but I'm sure we can convince them to give us a second chance."

"Lil would probably move here if it weren't for Jake," Zhang joked.

With a rumble of laughter, Rachid said, "Your parents are enough."

Zhang said, "I think it's hilarious that my mother is studying Arabic when she never learned English."

Rachid hugged his wife back into his chest and said, "She and my grandmother have been pretty inseparable since your parents moved in. I wonder if they will get along as well once they speak the same language."

With an amused glance back at her husband, Zhang asked, "What are you saying about my mother?"

Rachid laughed. "Nothing. I have to love her—she gave me you."

Zhang lightly tapped her husband's forearm. "Oh, sweet

words, but you can tell me the truth."

After a moment of thought, Rachid said, "Your mother is a strong, opinionated, stubborn woman. And so are you. I hope our daughters are as brave and loyal." He rubbed his chin on the top of his wife's head. "Although they will not be allowed to date... possibly ever."

"And our sons?" Zhang asked with a joking edge to her question.

"They will only be banned from attending American weddings."

"Because they might end up with someone like me?" Zhang challenged, some of the humor leaving her voice.

"There is no one else like you, Zhang." Rachid kissed her neck between each word.

"Our children will not be raised with a double standard."

"No, but they will be raised to respect the old ways as well as the new. As we do. It is a line we must all walk to belong. When you are out in the countryside, you curb your tongue and you dress as we dress. I know you do it out of respect for me, but it has also won you acceptance from my people."

Zhang sighed. "It's not always easy."

Pushing her hair back to expose her ear to his attention, Rachid said, "We could have left and made our home anywhere in the world. We still can if this is too much for you."

Hugging her husband's arms to her waist, Zhang said, "No, I see you show the same respect to my culture when we visit. You hold yourself differently and tone down the whole arrogant-prince act, and I know how hard that is for you. I'll survive."

Rachid growled, spun his wife in his arms and said, "Just survive?"

Zhang leaned against her husband and wiggled a bit until she felt him begin to stiffen. "Queen Zhang. It'll be difficult, but I'll manage somehow." A sudden thought flew into her passion-dazed brain. "Speaking of difficult, I'd like Jeremy to be part of the ground team when Proximus relocates here next month."

Rachid drew back and asked, "Why do we need a hacker?"

Zhang said, "He's a genius when it comes to firewalls and encryption." Rachid didn't look convinced. "And I owe him."

Frowning, Rachid responded, "We both do. What does he want?"

"He already has Corisi Enterprises and Andrade Global as clients. If he adds Proximus to his résumé there won't be a company in the world who won't bid for his services. He says becoming rich is part of his plan."

"Plan?"

"To win the heart of some woman."

Rachid kissed his wife's lips softy. "Then we'll hire him, because I cannot think of a more noble cause."

With a twinkle of mischief in her eyes, Zhang asked, "Do you think all this sweet talk will get you a new fantasy tonight?"

Rachid's eyebrows rose and fell suggestively. "You have more?"

Rising up onto her tiptoes, Zhang whispered into her husband's ear, "An infinite supply of them."

In one bold move, Rachid swung Zhang up into his arms, carried her through the suite and headed for the bedroom. "Then it is fortunate that we have a lifetime to explore them."

As Zhang sunk into the softness of the bed and pulled her eager new husband down on top of her, she thought, *I'm sorry I ever doubted you, Universe.*

The cosmos answered in a whisper that tickled her thoughts even as she started to lose herself to passion: *Boy or girl?*

It doesn't matter, Zhang answered and rolled on top of her husband, playfully trapping him beneath her. *I already have everything I need.*

So, four then.

Zhang paused and sat straight up on Rachid.

Four? I never said four.

"Are you okay?" Rachid asked, suddenly concerned.

Looking down at her husband, Zhang decided she was. She

kissed him and he forgot his question. *Sometimes when you lose to the universe, you win.*

Okay, four.

Better get started then.

The End

Can't wait to read the next book in the Legacy Collection?

Go to RuthCardello.com and add your email to the mailing list.

We'll send you an email as soon as
Rise of a Billionaire
is released!

Made in the USA
Middletown, DE
06 January 2023

21507087R00119